Christmas in Bar Harbor

MOUNT DESERT ISLAND SERIES

KATIE WINTERS

Chapter One

It was difficult to demand a stretch of good weather in Maine, particularly this early in May. Today, on graduation day of all days, the University of Maine architecture graduates stood out beneath shadowed skies and prayed the rain would hold out a little longer. Even still, as the northeastern wind ruffled their cobalt-blue graduation gowns threateningly, they stood with the resilience of students who'd taken the brunt of Maine weather the previous four years and lived to tell the tale. Rain, sleet, buckets of snowfall— it had all come after them. They'd still made it to graduation day. They'd still made it through.

Casey Harvey stood at the front of the line in preparation to be called out as the Top Architectural Student of the Graduating Class of 1996. Behind her, her rival, Gregory Pent, flashed her a sinister glare as he struggled to make peace with the few GPA points that separated them. The war was over. Casey was number one, and forever, Gregory would remain number two. That was that.

"It is my great pleasure to introduce you to a particularly gifted student here at the University of Maine." This was Casey's favorite professor, Professor Margorie Reynolds, a woman who'd single-handedly guided Casey over the previous four years to ensure she made appropriate decisions and joined the correct architectural programs — all in pursuit of the best-possible career. "She's been a stellar student and a remarkable young woman to know. We here at the University of Maine know she's off to create beautiful things. In the words of Frank Gehry, 'Architecture should speak of its time and place, but yearn for timelessness.' Casey knows her place in the timelessness of architecture—despite the finite nature of her time with us."

Casey shook her professor's hand as the crowd erupted with applause. Her eyesight blurred with tears, but she still managed to peer out to find her Aunt Tracy and sisters, Nicole and Heather, in the front row. Heather had declared her plan to arrive at the ceremony three hours early to get the "best seats in the house." It seemed like she'd managed it.

Casey lifted her diploma and waved it ever-so-slightly toward her beautiful family. Years before, they'd lost their mother, and their father had never been in the picture prior to his suicide. The foursome they'd created after their deaths, made up of Tracy, Casey, Nicole, and Heather offered all the love in the world they needed. Casey's heart lifted with love for them.

After the ceremony, Casey fell into the Harvey Girls' arms as they shrieked with excitement. Just above, the clouds burst apart, just as they'd promised they would, as raindrops fell over them. Heather yelped and leafed around her bag for an umbrella as Aunt

Tracy beckoned them toward the nearest doorway for cover. The University of Maine graduates rushed toward the closest shelter, their cobalt blue gowns ruffling out behind them. Heather burst into giggles at the sight.

"They look like panicked Smurfs," Heather teased.

"Four years of hard work, and all you can do is make fun of their outfits?" Nicole asked.

"A girl after my own heart," Casey returned brightly as Heather laughed even more. "Hey, I have to run back to the architecture office to pick up my backpack."

"Then we're going out to dinner, right?" Heather asked.

Casey rolled her eyes playfully. "I swear, you only came for the food afterward."

The hallways of the Architecture Building were grey and shadowed and quiet, a direct contrast to the previous four years of bustling students, wild gossip, and harried words of, "Did you get everything done on the homework? I need help!" Casey's heart lurched with sorrow. At no point throughout those four years had she thought any of it would ever be over. That was how time went.

Now, she had to figure out what came next. She'd applied to several jobs and had a range of job interviews over the next few weeks. None of them particularly illuminated her, although she knew she needed to count her blessings. Many of her co-graduates hadn't received so much as a telephone call back from their applications.

Once at the offices, Casey removed her graduation gown (although she had a hunch Heather would force it back on her at the restaurant if only to tease her more) and stuffed it in her backpack. She then donned her coat and swept out her dark brown locks across her back and shoulders. She recognized her own mother's face within the mirror on the far side of the architecture office and shivered at the sensation of always seeing Jane Harvey, just a little bit, within the creases of her aging face as time passed by.

"Casey? Is that you?" Professor Reynolds stepped out from her office with a mug of steaming tea. Her nose was ruby-red from the early May chill.

"Hi!" Casey's voice was overly bright with surprise. She swept a strand of hair behind her ear. "I thought everyone had already gone."

Professor Reynolds pressed her teeth onto her lower lip. "I'm glad to catch you. I just got a particularly interesting phone call. I thought of you immediately."

"Another job?" Professor Reynolds had been instrumental in pointing out the various Maine-based firms particularly interested in hiring new graduates like Casey.

"Not quite," Professor Reynolds affirmed. "I've noticed your lack of... shall we say... excitement? Surrounding these job interviews. I know you want to sink your teeth and talent into something particularly validating. And I think... well. I think this project is right up your alley."

Professor Reynolds showed Casey the notes she'd taken throughout the phone call. The gist was this. A very wealthy rancher in Montana wanted to build a brand-new, state-of-the-art ranch and mansion, one that suited his needs and illustrated him as the top rancher in at least the entire Western United States, if not the world.

"His name is Quintin Griffin," Professor Reynolds explained. "And he has a real love for great architecture. He references Frank Lloyd Wright and Philip Jonson and Gaudi, to name a few."

Casey chortled as her heart buzzed with excitement. "So you're suggesting I head over to Montana and build a Gaudi-inspired ranch?"

Although Casey's words had been in jest, Professor Reynolds nodded and said, "Why the heck not? It's never been done quite that way, has it?"

Casey arched an eyebrow as her curiosity mounted. "How would this even happen?"

"It's a contest," Professor Reynolds explained. "Entrants have the next four weeks to create their dream vision for the ranch. You then send the blueprints and a brief essay to Quintin Griffin, who will decide the winner. I can't possibly highlight just how excellent this opportunity is, Casey. The winner wouldn't just have the opportunity to build a truly spectacular architectural feat. Rather, the winner would be featured on countless architectural magazines and assuredly be touted as the next up-and-comer in the architecture world. You wouldn't be just another new face in the architecture world. You would be someone special. And if there's anything I truly believe about you, Casey, it's that you're something extraordinary."

Over the next two days, Casey went against her Aunt Tracy's suggestions and canceled every one of her upcoming architecture firm interviews. When they asked her why, she informed them that another opportunity had come up; this was, she supposed, truthful— although risky, since it wasn't like she was a shoo-in to win the contest. Thousands and thousands of other architecture rivals planned to enter. Why on earth would Quintin Griffin select her blueprints over theirs?

Due to money constraints, Casey returned to Aunt Tracy's house in Portland to remain honed in on the blueprints. Over the next three weeks, she fell into a state of hyper-focus, taking all her meals in her bedroom and visualizing her architectural plans at all times, even as she slept. During these weeks, she saw no friends and hardly accepted phone calls. Aunt Tracy once marveled, "How are you ever going to meet someone and settle down if..." But at this, Casey had countered, "Right, Aunt Tracy. After what my mother went through, it's not like I have any illusion that men are the secret ingredient to happiness." This had shut Aunt Tracy up for good.

Heather and Nicole both lived out on their own at this point but weaved in and out of Aunt Tracy's at-will. Frequently, they popped their heads into Casey's bedroom to say hello, but were usually met only with the hollowed-out eyes version of Casey. Heather called her the "architecture zombie." Nicole suggested she make herself sick if she didn't treat her mind and body better. Casey felt singularly focused on her mission.

The ranch itself spread out across her glorious page, with inspiration from countless of her favorite architects, yet with flairs all her own. Nobody could look at the blueprints and say, "Oh, this is a rip-off." No. They would look at it and say, "This is unique. This is never-before-seen. This is something truly spectacular."

The night before she sent off the blueprints and essay, she stumbled into the kitchen to find Heather, Nicole, and Aunt Tracy finishing up a beautiful home-cooked meal. Vegetarian was their frequent way when together (something Heather had started as a kid when she'd learned that meat came from animals), with homemade falafel and hummus. Casey's knees clacked together as she collapsed at the table and placed her cheeks in her hands.

"You look great," Heather joked as she poured a dollop more of olive oil into the hummus.

"Gee. Thanks," Casey returned.

"Seriously, Case, are you okay?" Nicole demanded.

"I don't know about this." Aunt Tracy scuttled back and forth at the countertop and then clacked four forks and four knives together at the kitchen table. "I read more about this rancher, Quintin."

"What about him?" Heather asked, her voice suddenly bright with the promise of gossip.

"Did you read that he could propel my career to the next level, just like that?" Casey asked as she snapped her fingers in the air.

"No. I read that he's the richest man in all of Montana and that he has an even bigger ego, to boot," Aunt Tracy returned.

"Not everyone can be completely kind and compassionate and good all the time. The world would be so boring," Casey snapped back. There it was again: her hot-headed tendency, which so often got her into trouble with her sisters, her aunt, and whatever boyfriend she had around at the time. Not many men stuck around, probably due to Casey's almost religious devotion to architecture (that and her sudden bursts of anger, which she couldn't fully control all the time).

Professor Reynolds had said Casey's anger was proof of her passion. But when it reared its ugly head and belittled people like her Aunt Tracy, who'd been nothing but generous and loving throughout Casey's entire life, Casey detested her propensity for anger and herself.

"Gosh, I'm sorry," Casey muttered immediately afterward as Aunt Tracy turned back toward the fridge.

"Come on, Casey. You need to eat a real meal and get a good night's sleep," Nicole offered softly.

"Did they tell you when they'll announce the contest results?" Heather asked.

Casey puffed out her cheeks. She detested the horrible, crashing weight of reality and preferred to be above a blank sheet, a pencil poised over it as she fleshed out a brand-new world within the realm of an architectural design.

"They didn't tell her," Aunt Tracy recited from the fridge.

Heather's eyes widened. "They're just going to make you wait?"

"Professor Reynolds told me about it," Casey grumbled. "She wouldn't lead me astray and besides. I have something here. I can feel it."

Heather and Nicole locked eyes over the table. Casey's stomach churned with anger. She yearned to ask just exactly what they shared within that exchanged glance, but decided instead to head back to her bedroom and finalize the last elements of the piece. Dinner could wait.

Heather walked Casey to the post office the following morning so that Casey could send the blueprints off with First Class Post. Heather dropped a quarter in the gum ball machine at the post office while Casey paid the exorbitant mail fare. When Heather returned to the counter, she flicked a yellow gum ball to and fro in her mouth like a child.

"Can't believe this yellow tube you're mailing across the country might be the key to your entire future," Heather said flippantly.

The postal worker eyed Casey and arched a brow toward her hairline. "Have you considered insurance?"

Casey cursed herself inwardly, considered the cost, and said, "No." After all, if the tube that held her blueprints didn't make it to Montana, then she'd be too late to enter the contest, anyway. It would be fate.

Heather had dreams of becoming a children's fantasy writer. On their walk back to their Aunt Tracy's place, she gabbed playfully about a story she wanted to write about a young woman who lived in a swamp and had dreams of grandeur. "You know, marrying the prince or going off to become a witch or something like that," Heather continued. "But when she leaves the swamp, her skin grows wrinkled and she becomes depressed and somber. She never imagined she'd miss the big, fat frogs or the ugly, twisted trees. Now, in the bright sun of the Montana plains..."

Casey stopped short at the intersection mere blocks from their house. "Heather, I know you're ridiculously creative and all that, but don't make me a sad, lonely woman on a Montana ranch in your story."

Heather grumbled inwardly. "I think you should have taken that job at the Portland architecture firm. What good is the rest of the world if your family isn't there with you?"

Casey bucked forward as a big truck barreled toward the intersection. The driver blared his horn as Casey and Heather shuffled forward. Heather cried out wildly as Casey shot her an angry look.

"Can you at least look for traffic?" Heather demanded.

"Listen, Heather. I've worked myself to death at architecture school. This is what I was born to do. If that takes me to Montana or Paris or Timbuktu, then I plan to head there to pursue my dream. I don't want you, Nicole or Aunt Tracy to hold me back. And I especially don't want you to guilt-trip me into staying."

Heather's face contorted with sorrow. They stopped at the opposite side of the road as Heather gasped for breath.

"I'm sorry, Casey. I am. I don't know why I said that."

Casey scuffed her toe against the sidewalk. It was impenetrably hot, an unusual thing for Maine, especially now at the very beginning of June. It felt as though nothing could ever return to the way it had been before.

"It's not like I want to leave my family," Casey breathed finally. "I just want to see what's out there. I want to see if I can make something of myself. Does that make any sense?"

Heather gripped Casey's wrist with thin yet firm fingers. Heather's ocean-blue eyes glittered with the soft light of the morning. "I'm being an idiot. I just want us always to be close. We've already lost so many people."

"You won't ever lose me," Casey told her as her throat tightened. "You know better than to think that will ever happen."

On the afternoon of the Fourth of July, Casey returned home from her summer job at the local pool, where she worked as a lifeguard in a bright-red swimsuit and an oversized baseball cap. She swept through the kitchen, where she found Heather, gabbing on the phone as usual, and Nicole painting her nails, a leg stretched out over the corner of the kitchen table. With Heather at age nineteen and Nicole at twenty, they still seemed to capture the perfect dynamic of American teenagers. Assuredly soon, the two of them would fall into whatever universe they would create for themselves

— with men or careers or babies. Time had its way with you, no matter what you did to keep it all the same. Casey knew that well. She learned it first hand when she'd watched her mother die.

Casey slipped into the fridge to grab a Diet Coke and then sauntered back toward the back deck, where she hoped to read the next issue of *Architecture Today* in relative peace. But before she could open the door, Heather hung up the phone and hollered, "You had a phone call earlier! Casey? He said it's urgent and wants you to call him back as soon as possible."

Casey grumbled as she turned back.

Nicole hooted and said, "Is it that guy you met at the pool the other day?"

Casey had been asked out on approximately four dates a week since her first day at the pool. They'd created a list of the idiotic pickup lines Casey had heard since then, which included: "Hey there, Sunshine. You're good enough to drown for. Reckon you could save my life?" and "Can I blow your whistle?"

"I never give these guys my number," Casey returned as she stepped back toward the phone.

"Not even that cute one? The football player?" Nicole asked.

"Especially not him... Harvard Elite? No thanks," Casey grumbled.

"Harvard Elite's not good enough for our Casey," Heather teased. "You know she's better than the most intelligent and handsome men in the country." She stuck out her tongue at Casey as Casey rolled her eyes into the back of her head.

Heather placed a finger on a little piece of scratch paper and pressed it across the counter for Casey to see. On the paper, Heather had written a phone number. "He had a hilarious accent. Like a drawl."

"Cute!" Nicole cried.

Casey rolled her eyes again. How could she begin to translate just how far away the concept of "love" was from her mind? Career came first. Everything else could fall into place later.

"Did he say what he wanted?" Casey demanded.

"A date with our big sis, that's what," Nicole returned as she finished off the red paint on her pinky nail.

"Actually, not even close, but he did say he was calling long-distance," Heather added as her eyes sparkled. "From Montana."

Casey's heart jumped into her throat. If there was ever a time for a full-blown heart attack, this was it. She gripped the paper and stared at the numbers before her, still in just her lifeguard swim-suit and a pair of ratty jean shorts.

Was this piece of paper her future?

Was this the next step of her life?

"Call him already!" Nicole cried from the kitchen table.

And so, Casey grabbed the receiver, lifted her finger, and punched out the numbers, one after another, until the phone rang out into the deep distance— across the Northeast, across the Midwest, until finally, it graced the gorgeous purple plains beyond.

Chapter Two

Casey's architectural blueprint became the most-talked-about thing across the North American continent, at least in architectural circles. Casey spotted her name on several magazines at the airport as she prepared to journey to that irrationally beautiful state. "The Next Frank Lloyd Wright?" One article wrote the words that made her stomach sizzle with adrenaline. Was it possible that all her dreams would soon come true?

It was now the end of July. It had been decided that Casey would come out to Montana to work alongside a more seasoned architect, along with a local construction firm. They would break ground on the ranch and neighboring mansion the second week of August, which would result in assuredly gut-busting, fourteen-hour workdays. "I'm not afraid of hard work," Casey had told Quintin Griffin over the phone. Immediately after, her bright tone of voice had made Quintin Griffin burst into laughter. She seemed so youthful, so free-spirited.

Oh, but she'd won the dang contest, hadn't she? So what if she seemed green sometimes?

"You know, I hand-selected your design after poring over four-hundred and seventy-seven documents," Quintin told her. "Yours was the work of a madwoman— a woman so utterly daring that even I couldn't believe what you'd crafted. You were the only one who managed to understand the assignment. And I cannot wait to piece through that brain of yours and really get to know you, Miss Harvey. I can't wait to see what comes out of this. Your career will change forever and my life? It will never be the same, either."

To Casey's surprise, Quintin Griffin sent a limo to the Bert Mooney Airport in Butte, Montana. Her sunglasses-wearing limo driver awaited her with a sign, on which he'd scribed the word: CASEY. It felt like something out of a silly book. Casey hustled toward the sign as her backpack shuffled across her shoulders.

"I can take your suitcase," the man told her.

But Casey didn't have a suitcase. None of the Harvey girls did, as they'd never had anywhere to go and had never had any money to get there. She pointed a thumb to her large backpack, which she'd stuffed to the gills with enough clothes to get her through two weeks. She had to guess that wherever she stayed had some kind of washing machine, or she would have to make her way to the nearest laundromat. It would be like college all over again.

"I see," the driver replied as he dragged her backpack off her shoulders and placed it delicately in the back of the limo, as though it were just as high-quality as a Gucci suitcase. He opened the door beside Casey and watched as she slid across the leather seats. Once latched up, she blinked up at him as her thoughts scurried around with excitement. The blue sky above seemed overly enormous, a large blue eggshell-colored half-orb above them. The driver noticed her gaze, turned his own eyes toward the blue sky, and muttered, "You're right. There isn't anything else like it in the world."

Quintin Griffin lived with his wife and their two daughters in a large house attached to his current ranch, located on the western side of the property on which they would soon break ground. The house was rather bland-looking, a bit neglected, with a large wrap-around fence that enclosed several brown and white and spotted horses, some of which tossed their heads wildly there beneath the sweltering haze of the sun.

He was something of a Montana cowboy. According to several newspaper articles that Casey had scrounged up at the library, Quintin had won a number of cowboy contests as a teenager and younger twenty-something before winning a number of gambling competitions, mainly for horse racing (although many journalists had a number of other ideas about where that gambling money came from). This money had allowed him to purchase the ranch and become a top player in the ranching industry in Montana. Casey had kept this information away from Aunt Tracy, as Aunt Tracy wouldn't have felt very good about sending her eldest niece off to work alongside a man with such "loose" morals.

Quintin Griffin was only twenty-nine years old. This was a surprise to Casey, especially as it seemed he'd already lived more lives than most men managed in several decades. He stepped out of his house in a cowboy hat and a dark navy blue button-down shirt and a pair of blue jeans and placed his hands on his hips. Casey stood in the driveway as the limo driver scooped her backpack from the back. The two assessed one another until Quintin let out a wild laugh.

"There she is. The architectural genius!"

Casey smirked as her stomach twisted with fear and excitement. "You flatter me."

"And is flattery so bad?" Quintin asked with a drawl.

"Only when it's used for manipulation," Casey told him.

"And what's so bad about manipulation?" Quintin teased right back. He lifted the edge of his cowboy hat higher to allow for their eyes to meet. "Now, why don't you come on in and meet my family? We have several things to get to and a number of things to build. But right now, we've got a classic meal to prepare for you. And I have a hunch you'll love my little girls."

Casey was surprised to find that Quintin Griffin's often-talked-about ego was quickly sedated for the purpose of friendly conversation and a good, honest meal. Once inside, he informed her that they had a no-shoes policy throughout the house. Casey slipped off her hole-filled tennis shoes and followed him in mismatched socks, all the way to the dining room, where his two little girls, Izzy and Frankie, sat with their legs dangling down from the oversized chairs. His wife, Henrietta, greeted Casey warmly with a kiss on the cheek. She was perhaps a few years older than Quintin, which was a surprise, yet her smile was youthful and warm.

"Quintin just hasn't shut up about that design of yours," she said, offering a similar drawl. "But I hope you know you're not just making an architectural feat. Two little girls, and maybe more, will grow up there. It's primarily a family home."

Casey hadn't accounted for that when she'd made the plans. Her eyes twitched toward Quintin's as the air around them shifted awkwardly. He guffawed and then said, "Henrietta, you know our girls will just love living there. It'll be like living in a fantasy land."

Henrietta grumbled something before she turned back toward

the kitchen to fetch the rest of the dinner, which she'd assuredly prepared over the previous few hours. Quintin's cheek twitched.

"And where is your Uncle Grant?" he boomed to his daughters.

"Uncle Grant is checking on the sick horse," Izzy informed. "He said he'll be right back."

Quintin made his way toward the window to peer out across the fields. He clucked his tongue, then turned back to catch Casey's eye. They glittered with the soft light of the early evening. "My brother came to stay with us a few months ago. One hell of a rider. He hasn't had as much luck as me in the old money department, so I'm giving him a leg up while he plans out his life."

Behind Quintin, Casey caught sight of a youthful cowboy in a pair of shabby-looking cowboy boots. He spread a large hand across the broad neck of a beautiful auburn horse. It seemed as though the horse and the cowboy were in perfect communion as the orange orb of sun stewed over the horizon line behind them. It seemed like an overly nostalgic painting of a forgotten time.

"He liked your design, too, although he did mention several times that he didn't 'get it,' whatever that means," Quintin said brightly.

Grant Griffin strolled up to the large house just as Henrietta reappeared with a large basket lined with a thick towel, upon which she'd dotted several buttery rolls. "Fresh from the oven," she announced, avoiding Casey's eyes.

Years later, Casey wasn't entirely sure what she and Grant first said to one another there in the dining room of the soon-to-be-abandoned first family home of his brother, the wealthy rancher, Quintin Griffin. Sometimes, to her sisters, Casey insisted that Grant started with, *"Aren't you a little young to be an architect?"*

17

But Grant always said this wasn't true. "I just said, *'Hey there! Welcome to Montana!'*" In any case, one thing Casey remembered was that when Grant walked into the dining room, she felt something she'd never felt before— something pure and honest and authentic. Something that told Casey, beyond the realm of her architectural plans and breaking ground on the ranch, that her life was about to change.

Casey was no imbecile. She wasn't the sort of woman to get all swept up in a romance when she had a job to do. In fact, over the next several months, Casey dug herself deep into the task-at-hand — developing a very beautiful and layered relationship with the other, more-experienced architect and single-handedly managing a number of construction meetings herself.

It wasn't until late October, beneath the Montana sky, black as ink yet littered with glorious stars, that Grant Griffin and Casey Harvey found themselves alone. It had been months of strange eye contact and whispered words. Hope had knocked around at the base of Casey's belly, sometimes making her so dizzy that she hadn't been able to eat.

Late October and more than three months after her arrival.

And suddenly, Casey found herself tipping her chin skyward to allow Grant Griffin to kiss her tenderly for the first time.

She'd never been kissed like this before. It was unquestioned. It made every other kissing experience lackluster and forgettable.

This cowboy, this man before her— he was and would be everything to her. She would never feel like this again. She knew it the way you know rain's about to cascade down from a darkening cloud.

"You're impossible, you know that?" he told her after their kiss.

"I've heard this suggested before," Casey replied coyly before he kissed her all over again. A moment later, her knees eventually collapsed. Grant caught her just in the nick of time. He pressed Casey against him, his thick arms wrapping around her in a cradle position. For months, she'd felt like a pillar of strength and intellect and architectural know-how. But just then, she felt like a woman.

She rather liked the feeling.

Casey returned home for Thanksgiving and Christmas before returning to the ranch to continue the project. Quintin hadn't sent a limo to pick her up upon her return to Montana. Rather, Grant's now-familiar pick-up truck hummed out front, a sight that made Casey's heart nearly burst from her chest. She flung her arms around him and allowed him to whip her around and around in circles as she shrieked with joy. Nobody looking on would have thought, *"There she is. One of the most promising young women in the architecture world right now."* No. All they would have said was, *"There's a cowboy and his beautiful girl."*

Casey now balanced out her days like this: ten to twelve hours with the construction workers, other architects, or Quintin Griffin himself. The other hours were spent almost exclusively with Grant, who took her on long and beautiful horse rides, showing her the ragged edges of the mountain ranges and the wild animals that lingered across the horizon line. Casey, who'd always labeled herself a Maine girl and only a Maine girl, found herself falling head-over-heels for Montana.

Just as Professor Reynolds had suggested, the week that the ranch and mansion finalized construction, *Architecture Today* featured Casey Harvey on the cover. Grant purchased twenty-five copies and arranged an enormous celebration at the ranch, both to celebrate the opening and Casey's success. Quintin's boisterous and drunk nature led him to say to Casey, *"You're the best thing that's happened to this family,"* around eight in the evening. Then, later on in the evening, he said, *"You idiot. You destroyed the night,"* to his wife, Henrietta, who'd only spilled a bit of white wine on his button-up.

"My brother has several problems," Grant confessed to Casey deep into that night. "He helps me out a great deal, that's true. But his mental health has never been great. He's rash and he's arrogant. He's had a lot of luck so far. I just worry that one day, the luck will run out."

Casey hadn't consumed anything at all throughout the party. In fact, she hadn't had any alcohol since three weeks earlier, when she'd noticed that something with her body was amiss. Now, with countless job offerings sputtering in from all over the continent, she was faced with the ultimate question: what should she do with her life? And who did she want to build that life with?

"Grant. I'm pregnant," she whispered now, as the Montana stars sparkled above them.

Grant's lips parted in surprise. "You're kidding."

She shook her head vehemently as she laced her fingers through his. "I've never felt like this before, not with anyone."

"I haven't either, Casey. You've changed my world."

Casey closed her eyes against the weight of this truth. How could she allow someone to love her like this, to truly love her? Did she even deserve it?

"I want to take the big position at the architecture firm in Portland," she said finally. "I need to be by my sisters. They're my world. And there's no way, in my mind, that my baby won't know them and love them the way I do."

Grant's eyes shimmered with a mix of sorrow and excitement.

"I know that I'm asking you to give up your greatest love," she continued hurriedly. "I know I'm asking you to step away from the ranch. But Grant, I promise you. We can come out here all the time. I think I can negotiate around a million vacation days a year."

Grant chuckled. "After that article in *Architecture Today*, I reckon you can negotiate anything."

Casey's grin widened as her eyes filled with tears. Grant shuddered and sighed.

"You're telling me that I'm going to be a dad."

Casey laughed outright. "That's exactly what I'm telling you."

Grant stretched his fingers across her cheeks as his eyes widened. "You're impossibly beautiful and intelligent and far, far too good for me, Casey Harvey. I will love you and this baby as long and as well as I can. And we won't do it here. We'll do it in Maine. I know that your heart will forever be in Maine. Let's go. Together."

Chapter Three

Present Day

The Keating House on the outer edge of the family property overlooked Frenchman Bay, which frothed with violent waves beneath an impenetrably black and starless sky. Casey hovered at the kitchen's bay window with a wine glass lifted as her younger sister, Heather, padded around in thick wool socks behind her. It was the night before Thanksgiving, and, as always, there was so much to do before the big celebration.

"I just don't know how I managed to do that," Heather grumbled inwardly as she tossed the blackened pie crust into the trash can. She then poured herself another glass of Primitivo wine, leaned against the counter, and took a long, exaggerated sip.

"No chance the wine consumption hindered your pie crust efforts?" Casey teased.

Heather rolled her eyes back as a smile swelled between her

cheeks. "Just keep this between us, please and thank you. Now that Nicole is an expert chef, I'm pretty intimidated."

Casey, Heather, and Nicole's children had gathered to gossip and drink wine, spirits, and beer in the living room. The stereo thumped with a modern song that both Casey and Heather now admitted they'd never heard before. Nicole remained at the Keating Inn and Acadia Eatery for the night, finalizing the dinner rush with Luke, the sous chef and Heather's soon-to-be boyfriend, by her side. Now, Heather's twin daughters, Kristine and Bella, sang along brightly to the song while Donnie, Casey's son, whooped and hollered.

"I didn't realize we started a fraternity house," Heather teased.

"You didn't know? That's why I put the kegs out back," Casey shot back a moment later. "Maybe in a little while, we can hold each other's legs into the air for a round of keg stands."

"Sounds like a blast, Case," Heather returned with a wink. "If only you hadn't been so hyper-focused on architecture school during college. I have a hunch you've never done a keg stand in your life."

"And gosh, I just know that I really missed out on something..." Casey returned. Her voice was heavy with sarcasm. "Oh, woe is me. I never did a keg stand..."

"Mom? What are you talking about?" Casey's daughter, Melody, now hovered in the doorway between the living room and the kitchen with an empty glass of wine lifted in the air. She was twenty-four years old, with dark curly hair and bright blue eyes, inherited from her father's genes.

"Your mom was just saying how much she wants to binge drink in the backyard," Heather countered as she fluttered flour over a cutting board in preparation to make a whole new pie crust.

"I was not," Casey quipped. "How's it going in the living room?"

"Oh, fine," Melody offered as her smile widened. "Just came for a fill-up."

Heather passed Melody the bottle of Primitivo, which was coated in flour. "I meant to ask you more about your business, Melody. How did everything come together?"

Melody worked as an art dealer and interior designer for wealthy people in several cities across the country. Casey's heart swelled with pride. It seemed that Melody had gotten that "artistic eye" from Casey. She'd been featured in several magazines and online articles, all of which called Melody Griffin one of the most sought-after interior designers from Los Angeles to New York City and beyond.

"It was the strangest thing," Melody started as she lifted her glass toward her lips. "I was twenty-one years old at some party in a high-rise apartment building in the Upper West Side. Some guy I'd met at a bar had invited me, even though I told him I was only there on spring break."

"Some guy?" Heather asked now with a laugh. "It's funny how guys of our past somehow become 'some guy' to us later, isn't it?"

Melody chuckled good-naturedly. "Sure. Yeah, I don't even know if I could pick him out in a crowd. But at the party, I got to talking to the hostess, a woman named Janine Potter, who said she was hungry for new kinds of art to fill her apartment with. Artists who hadn't been seen before. Artists who made her think in ways she didn't know she could think. I was friendly with a few lesser-known Brooklyn artists, and I suited her up with a few pieces—for a pretty price, you can imagine. She told all her rich friends about me, and they went on to tell their friends. By the time I graduated from college, I really didn't even need the degree."

"We're just so proud of you, sweetheart," Heather said as she spread her hands out over the rolling pin and pressed it over the dough. "It reminds me so much of your mother when she was twenty-one, twenty-two. She was just so devoted to her craft— to her art. You really couldn't get her out of her room if she was hyper-focused on something."

Casey's stomach tightened. Melody gave her mother a curious glance before she shifted back toward the doorway.

"What time is Dad getting in tomorrow?" Melody asked as her tone grew brighter, falser.

"Not quite sure, honey. I guess he'll call me sometime tonight to give me more of the details," Casey offered.

Melody's chin quivered strangely. "I can't remember the last time I saw him. Our work schedules just haven't aligned that well."

Casey's heart felt cracked. She wanted to articulate to Melody just how little she'd seen Grant Griffin over the past year, as well, but didn't want to worry her. Even at twenty-four, Melody remained Melody, Casey and Grant's sweet-faced little girl, who they would do anything to protect. What she didn't know about Grant's staggering number of absent days in Casey's life wouldn't hurt her.

"He works hard. You both do," Casey told her daughter.

"It's good he'll be here for Thanksgiving," Heather said firmly. "Because I'm pretty sure he's the only one who likes pecan pie. And for some reason, I've made two of them."

Melody hurried back to the living room, where Nicole's daughter and son, Abby and Nate, had sprung into a duet of their own. It seemed like a family-style karaoke session, with no signs of stopping any time soon.

Heather's ocean-blue eyes found Casey's through the puff of flour between them.

"He is coming. Isn't he?" Heather whispered.

Casey grunted inwardly. "Of course. He's never missed Thanksgiving."

Heather's face contorted strangely. It looked as though she grappled with what she wanted to say and how to say it, all in fear of Casey's hot-headed nature. Before Casey lost her temper, she dismissed herself and shuffled up the staircase toward the bedroom she'd taken as her own.

Several weeks ago, Nicole had called Casey and asked her if she had a bit of spare time to help out at the Keating Inn and Acadia Eatery. At the time, Nicole's daughter, Abby, had been crashing at Casey's place, as she'd lost her job in Providence and hadn't known how to re-connect with her mother. Casey, whose heart had ached with loneliness as Grant had paraded his new, flashy career across the continent, had welcomed Abby with open arms. She had cooked her breakfast, lunch, and dinner, given her thoughtful responses as she'd spiraled about her "failed" career (at her age, failure wasn't an option— it was just a stepping stone to something greater), and kept her secret safe regarding her whereabouts. When she had informed Abby of her plans to head to Bar Harbor, of all places, Abby had initially resented this. Now, Abby flourished as one of the most important pieces of the ever-churning mechanism of the Keating Inn and Acadia Eatery. It was now a family affair in every single way.

Ironically, this was probably what Adam Keating had wanted all along.

All her life, Casey had only known to brew with hatred for her father, Adam Keating. The story she'd been told was that he'd left Jane behind with three little girls before taking his own life in Bar Harbor. Now, part of that story had been debunked — but the story still didn't come out in Adam Keating's favor. Instead, it seemed that Adam had fallen head-over-heels for some other Bar Harbor woman. He'd left Casey and brand-new baby, Nicole, which had led Jane to run back to her home of Portland to raise Casey and Nicole with her sister, Aunt Tracy. Almost immediately afterward, Adam's new wife gave birth to Heather— who wasn't Adam's baby at all. After the woman left Adam and baby Heather in the lurch, Adam passed off Heather to poor Jane, with a *"Sorry, I'm an awful human being"* sentiment.

It was a huge colossal mess. And strangely enough, Heather, Nicole, and Casey had found beauty in it. Under their ownership, the Keating Inn and Acadia Eatery had flourished. Nicole had rekindled her desire to become head chef, and Heather had discovered the truth of her lineage (for better or for worse).

Casey removed her blue jeans and blouse in her bedroom and blinked at her reflection. There she was again: Jane Harvey, or someone rather like Jane Harvey, with fine lines around her eyes and even crisper ones across the forehead. Casey was now forty-seven years old— with very little to show for it. She hadn't seen her husband in months. Her career had ended abruptly a few years before.

All that work. All that love. What had it all been for? Had it been for this, to work at the front desk of the Keating Inn and

Acadia Eatery? Had she really torn herself apart to work in hospitality?

She collapsed at the desk and peered down at the blueprints she'd crafted over the previous weeks. She had an image of a second house on the property, off to the west of the main Keating house, with two stories, a spacious attic that acted as a library, four bedrooms, and a massive kitchen with enough space for plenty of family gatherings. It was the first blueprint she'd drawn up in over five years. During the first hours of the drawing process, she had audibly wept.

If there was something she could understand about the story of Adam Keating, it was this: life never turned out the way you planned.

Or, to quote John Lennon, "Life is what happens when you're busy making other plans."

Casey lifted an eraser to the outer edge of the plan and scrubbed it across several imperfect lines. With a delicate motion, she finalized the corner of the porch. As she drew, she could visualize the space so particularly, right down to how the sunlight would stream in through the windows. From this porch, whoever sat would be able to see the porch of the house she was designing. She imagined them waving to one another as the morning light shimmered through the trees that separated them.

Casey grew lost in her work, something she'd forgotten she could do. Time held no meaning. When she did glance up at the clock on the wall, she was shocked to find it was already eleven at night. Downstairs, the kids raged on with their karaoke tunes.

On the other side of the continent, it was only eight in the evening.

Casey grabbed her cell. As the call rang out across the lakes, plains, and mountains, she gripped one post of the four-poster bed, her knuckles skeletal-white. It wasn't like him to say he'd call and not call. Or was it?

Grant didn't answer. Casey's stomach tightened with a mix of fear and embarrassment. Should she try again? There was a possibility he was in the shower. Or at a business dinner. Or he'd forgotten his phone in his hotel room when he headed to the gym.

He was in Los Angeles this week, wasn't he? He'd shared a work calendar with her several years ago but often forgot to update it, as his schedule shifted so frequently. Besides, at a certain point, Casey had stopped checking it as much as she used to because it didn't matter if Grant was in Seattle or Austin or Orlando. Wherever he was, he wasn't there with her.

And perhaps he'd set up his life that way on purpose.

Casey collapsed again at the desk and placed her hands on either side of the blueprint. Although this house-setting wasn't anything ultra-impressive (it wouldn't be discussed in *Architecture Today*... that was for sure), she still felt proud of it. It would house her dearest loved ones. It would play witness to countless bouts of laughter. Perhaps it would host her grandchildren's first steps. She remembered again what her eventual sister-in-law, Henrietta, had said that very first day she'd arrived in Montana. "My girls will grow up in that house." Back then, Casey hadn't thought of architecture that way. She'd thought of it only as pushing limits. She'd thought of it as the ultimate modern art.

Casey walked back down to the kitchen, where she found a near-perfect twin-set of apple pies upon the counter. Heather had managed the crusts without char. Casey poured herself a full glass of wine as Kristine and Bella performed a gut-wrenching performance of Sinead O'Conner's "Nothing Compares 2 U" in the living room, between giggle-fits. It was strange to think that their father, Max, had disappeared out to sea a year and a half ago, already. It was stranger, still, to believe that Grant Griffin had borderline disappeared, himself— by choice. People came and went. Why did Casey ever think you could hold onto any sort of happiness?

On second thought, she gripped the neck of the open wine bottle and carried it up the steps along with her. Nobody noticed her brief sojourn to the kitchen. Nobody cared.

Back in the bedroom, she drank and burrowed herself into her emerging emotions, which were every which way as her sorrows grew. How would she explain to Melody and Donnie that their father no longer wanted to spend holidays with them? How would she explain that their father made almost no effort to include Casey in his life any longer? How?

Grant had nabbed a job right after his arrival to Maine a little more than twenty-four years ago. It had been at a local mechanic's, where he'd worked with his hands and became a welcome new smile in a tight-knit community in Portland. After Melody was born, Grant took time off to raise Melody, as Casey's career was like a rocket; such was its force. She took jobs worldwide, from Tokyo to Buenos Aires to Denver to Boston. She arranged it so that she was the only creative talent and wasn't required to spend much time at the building sites themselves. This allowed Grant, Casey, and Melody plenty of family time— something they enjoyed so much that they welcomed Donnie into the fold only a year later. (Best to just get all the baby stuff out of the way, they'd told each other. They'd never envisioned how much they'd miss baby time later on.)

Throughout those early years of Casey's high-powered career and their babies' first stages, Grant never showed any annoyance. He photographed beautiful moments in his children's lives to allow for gorgeous scrapbooking, writing out "Melody's first word — Dada (sorry, Casey :P)," and "Donnie's first steps - October 17, 1999."

When Grant had announced the job interview at the sales firm, Casey had simply congratulated him and then jumped in the car to take Donnie to soccer practice. She'd never envisioned that that job interview would become the gateway to all this. Grant had climbed the corporate ladder and become an absolute all-star in the sales community— something not entirely surprising, as he was still that crooked-smiled cowboy, who she'd fallen in love with all those years ago.

But with his power, responsibility had ballooned. And in the previous year of Casey's life, she'd spent almost half the year sleeping next to him, if that.

Something was wrong. When Nicole and Heather inquired about Grant and her marriage, Casey would make a joke, or she would shove the topic aside. It was akin to staring at the sun.

Now, it felt as though she hid in Bar Harbor— from her life with Grant and also from the fact that, over five years ago, she had quit her high-powered architecture job after a particularly heinous argument with several of her colleagues. They'd accused her of hot-headedness. They'd accused her of "losing her edge." Horrific words had spewed between the lot of them. And Casey, eternally proud, almost always to a fault, had said, *"Go to hell,"* and marched out of the same office she'd once designed.

The phone blared out even before Casey had a firm grip on what she did now. She staggered toward the black square of window, which again offered a gorgeous view of Frenchman Bay, where a single, tiny boat floated out far beyond and blinked its confident lights.

"Hello?" said a groggy voice. What time was it, now?

"Good evening," Casey blared, slurring the words together.

"Good evening? It's two in the morning," the voice returned. "And this is... Oh, gosh. Mrs. Griffin. Did you call me by accident?"

Casey refused to glance at herself in the mirror. She had a hunch the sight of herself, now— a drunken, sorrowful, lonely woman, who'd once had it all, would destroy her.

"Yes. Hello, Stacy. I'm so sorry to call you at home, but I had no choice." Casey's throat tightened. "I wondered if you could tell me if my husband's business calendar is correct. I thought he was in Los Angeles this week with plans to fly to Massachusetts tomorrow morning. But there's no flight listed and..."

Stacy, Grant's secretary, giggled sleepily. The noise made Casey freeze with fear. In her previous dealings with Grant's secretary, she'd been formal and polite, if a bit air-headed. Casey had longed to ask Grant why he'd selected such an attractive secretary for the position, but had reasoned that it wasn't like he spent much time in the office, anyway. Besides, she hated the idea of herself as the traditional jealous housewife. She'd never planned to be a house-wife. She'd planned to build the house herself!

"Excuse me?" Casey demanded of Stacy.

"I'm sorry..." Stacy tried to recover. "I really am."

"I just need a bit of information from you," Casey declared. "If you could pull yourself together."

There it was: her hot-headed nature. *Why couldn't she control herself?*

"Mrs. Griffin, I don't know what you want me to say," Stacy returned.

Casey's heart dropped into her belly. "I told you. I just need to know if my husband has plans to fly to Massachusetts. I want to make sure we know when to expect him for Thanksgiving dinner."

"Thanksgiving dinner!" Stacy cackled, as though the concept was far beyond anything she'd ever envisioned. "Oh, Mrs. Griffin."

Casey's opinion of herself had fallen nearly to zero over the previous few years, especially since she'd walked out of the architecture firm she'd built from the ground up. The fact that her husband seemed to avoid her like the plague hadn't helped things. Now, this Stacy's giggling was the nail in the coffin.

"Give me an answer, Stacy. Or I'll have some serious words with my husband about your qualifications for this position," Casey blared.

Stacy's laughter grew increasingly high-pitched. "Oh, Casey, honey. I used to look up to you! Gosh. It's funny to think of that now. It's funny to think of so much. Suffice it to say, but there's a whole lot about your husband that you don't know about. Suffice it to say— there's a whole lot you'll never really know."

Then, she hung up.

Chapter Four

The Keating House, although significant, wasn't quite big enough to host the entire Harvey Sisters' families within its walls comfortably. This meant that the living area was something like a slumber party, with Nate and Melody stretched out on both couches and Donnie sleeping peacefully on a blow-up mattress. Around five in the morning on Thanksgiving Day, a half-drunk and dehydrated Casey paused in the doorway of the living room. She peered down at the three sleeping bodies and the leftover chaos of the cousin party, with multiple stacks of red solo cups and wine-tinged glasses and even a few shot glasses scattered about. Melody groaned in her sleep and tossed over on her side, taking a large chunk of brunette curls along with her. Casey hurried around them and dove into the soft light of the kitchen, where she brewed a pot of coffee and hovered again at the bay window, rubbing her palms together distractedly.

Sleep hadn't come for her. She imagined it never would again.

"There's a whole lot about your husband that you don't know."

The words rang through Casey's mind as the coffee pot gurgled and spat. The words had opened up a vast ocean between herself and her husband. There was no telling how deep the lies went. There was no telling what other secrets lurked in the depths.

Since Max's disappearance, Heather had struggled going out on the water, knowing that the ocean had ultimately taken his life. The ocean between Casey and Grant was a far different sort— yet it had a similar strength.

Had Casey ever believed that she and Grant told one another everything? No. She never had. It was essential to human relationships to keep something for yourself to not lose who you are. This was something she'd believed in totally, especially as she'd learned about her mother's dedication to Adam Keating and how that had made her struggle. For this reason, Casey had been careful to nourish the small and unique moments of individuality she'd had, especially earlier in her career.

If a man flirted with Casey at work, she would have enjoyed it because it would have been a moment when she would be seen as an attractive individual rather than a member of a couple. When the kids had been a little bit older, she'd taken brief trips, all to herself, during which she'd dreamed up new architectural designs and lived in the imaginative echoing of her head. She'd told Grant he could take those alone times, too— but at that time, he hadn't made his own money and probably, felt guilty about taking "time off." Time off from what? He might have asked.

Perhaps it had been necessary when he'd discovered his way forward, for him to travel long and far if only to discover his true self again. But what had he kept from Casey over the years? Had he crossed the lines of fidelity? Had he fallen out of love?

These were difficult questions, especially at five-fifteen in the morning on Thanksgiving.

Casey sipped from her mug of coffee as she toiled through her headache. Nicole stumbled into the kitchen at five forty-five and switched on the lights. She nearly jumped from her skin at the sight of Casey, there alone in the shadows of the kitchen.

"What are you doing here?" she asked, still half asleep.

"I couldn't sleep," Casey replied with a shrug. "Can you turn off the lights?"

Nicole turned them off again and hovered in the soft light of the early morning with her arms dangling on either side of her. Her lips erupted with a yawn as she explained the frantic nature of the previous evening.

"I just can't understand why everyone at the Eatery was out of their minds hungry the night before Thanksgiving, but we were stuffed to the gills till around ten-thirty at night. After that, we had everyone lying around until eleven-thirty. Luke had to kick everyone out at twelve-forty-five. I collapsed on my back in my chef whites."

Casey laughed appreciatively and patted the space on the table across from her. "Take a load off. We have a long day ahead of us."

"Thank goodness Heather made the rest of the pies," Nicole noted as she shuffled toward the table.

Casey pressed her lips together, holding in the story of Heather's initial pie crust failure. Nicole didn't need more stress.

"What time is Grant getting in today?" Nicole asked as she suppressed another yawn.

"Around one or so, I think," Casey lied. "But we shouldn't

wait for him if he doesn't make it before the big meal. He said he'd grab leftovers."

"All right. Well, that's too bad. He really should have planned to get here last night," Nicole said pointedly. "Plus, traveling on Thanksgiving can be so harried— all those grumpy people trying to get to their families in time."

"I've seen *Planes, Trains, and Automobiles* if that's what you're referring to." Casey was surprised she could still tease Nicole, despite the aching of her heart.

Nicole laughed. "I forgot about that. Remember how Aunt Tracy used to watch that every year?"

"She was obsessed with John Candy," Casey said.

"Gosh, we should really make the kids watch it in her memory," Nicole offered sadly. "I can't believe how long she's been gone now." She furrowed her brow, then added, "I told you that the first time I ever met Uncle Joe was on Thanksgiving, right?"

Casey shook her head. "You didn't. Was that when you snuck around, coming to Bar Harbor and telling us you were off somewhere else?" Casey had long since given up her anger surrounding Nicole's departure from Portland to Bar Harbor. What did it matter, now? It had now become their home.

"Yes. Uncle Joe opened his world to me. I've never forgotten it," Nicole murmured. "I'm trying to remember where you were. Probably Montana, right?"

Casey nodded as her eyes glistened with tears. "We often went to the ranch for Thanksgiving."

"So Grant didn't want to this year? Or you told him that we had to do it here? I mean, we've had quite the year. It's important that we come together for this," Nicole pointed out.

Casey hadn't had any kind of conversation around it. She'd

simply said, *"I'm in Bar Harbor. Are you coming for Thanksgiving?"* And he'd said, *"Sure."*

"He gets it," Casey told her.

Nicole nodded. "He always did. Gosh, I was envious of you two when you first had Melody and Donnie. A stay-at-home dad! Michael was such a jerk during those early years. I couldn't get him to stay home with Abby and Nate to save my life. Not even so I could go get my haircut."

Casey grumbled inwardly. Michael had been a scumbag of the highest order. When he'd left her and their children for a younger woman and run off to build a brand-new life with a brand-new baby, they hadn't yet known that his actions had echoes of Adam Keating. How easy it was for men. Often, they aged like a fine wine and became even more enticing to young women, while the wives they left behind had to face the world armed only with night creams and whatever beauty treatments their wallets allowed for.

In Nicole's case, of course, she had run off and built her beautiful career as head chef at Acadia Eatery. Beyond that, she'd recently became "friends" with the town's greatest villain, Evan Snow, who frequently took her on dinner "non-dates" and called her to talk for hours.

A little while later, Heather joined them at the kitchen table with a mug of coffee. Half-moon shadows beamed out from beneath her eyes as she told them that Kristine and Bella had gossiped with her late into the night about their recent boy troubles.

"I'm so glad they want to tell me everything," Heather muttered. "But right now, I wish that 'everything' had a little less to it, so I could get some more sleep."

"When you're twenty-two, you don't need sleep," Casey

affirmed, remembering her wild nights over her blueprints. "Your body is a well-oiled machine."

"Not so well-oiled these days, I'm afraid," Heather said with a laugh. "Although I guess some Bailey's in the coffee might help."

"It's Thanksgiving, after all," Nicole pointed out brightly as she leaped up and grabbed the Bailey's from the fridge. "I was thinking I would get the cinnamon roll dough from the fridge and bake them for the kids and us."

"Luke might stop by earlier if there are cinnamon rolls." Heather's eyes glittered with excitement.

"Oh?" Nicole made a funny noise in the back of her throat. "I forgot to mention, maybe, that Evan's two eldest children won't be able to make it for Thanksgiving. I told him and Maddy to come around whenever they like."

Heather dropped a hand over her mouth, ever over-dramatic. These were not Casey's genes, she recognized now with an inward laugh.

"What?" Nicole demanded of Heather.

Heather rolled her eyes excitedly. "Come on, Nicole. You're having a guy over for Thanksgiving."

"It's just Evan Snow," Nicole countered. "He almost destroyed the Inn a month ago."

"Oh, he did not, and you know it," Heather retorted. "He was instrumental in ensuring that we stayed open."

Nicole's cheeks flashed pink. Her cleansed hands drew out dollops of cinnamon roll dough, then folded and dropped them with a funny flop on the baking sheet. "I told you again and again. We're just friends."

"Kristine might have mentioned she saw you guys the other day," Heather said as her voice lowered.

Nicole twisted herself around as her eyes widened. "What are you talking about?"

At this, Heather cackled until her body shook. "I'm just kidding! Kristine didn't see anything. Although from your expression, I have to believe... that something did happen?"

Nicole turned back toward her dough and muttered, "Nothing happened. Nothing at all."

Casey and Heather exchanged mischievous looks. Casey shook her head ever-so-slightly. It was best to tread lightly so as not to frighten Nicole. If she wanted to fall in love, she had to do it on her terms, slowly. It didn't matter if the man in question was Evan Snow or the Easter Bunny. Casey and Heather had to be supportive.

Luke walked into the Keating House mere minutes after Nicole removed the first batch of cinnamon rolls from the oven. He pulled off his winter hat and spread out his arms wide in greeting, taking up the whole of the kitchen doorway.

"There they are! The Harvey Sisters! Happy Thanksgiving!" he cried.

"Are you drunk?" Casey teased.

"I am. Just a little," Nicole shot back as she lifted the bottle of Bailey's.

Heather leaped from the kitchen table and wrapped her arms around Luke's chest as she gazed into his beautiful eyes. Casey's heart thumped strangely in her chest. She felt like an extra in a film while her sisters had the major starring roles. She wasn't even sure she would have a speaking part in this scene. Her character had nothing to do or say. She knew her insecurities were getting the best of her.

One by one, Nicole, Casey, and Heather's children arose like zombies, grunting and scratching as they entered the kitchen to collect mugs of coffee and hot, gooey cinnamon rolls. Melody swept down to place a kiss on Casey's cheek as Donnie tore off a large chunk of his sugary pastry with his teeth. He looked too much like his father when Casey met him, with his crooked smile and broad shoulders. When they'd journeyed to Montana together, Grant had been grateful that both Donnie and Melody had taken to horseback riding with zeal. Of Donnie, he'd said, *"He's even more of a natural than I ever was, I swear."* Casey had wondered at the time if there was regret tied up in Grant's words. Had he hated raising their children away from Montana?

"When's Dad getting in?" Donnie asked as he hovered by the counter.

"Didn't you say around one?" Nicole chimed in as she turned to face Casey.

"I can't wait to meet him," Luke offered. "I think Donnie and Nate can back me up here when I say we need more men around the house."

"When one of you men can bake cinnamon rolls as good as this, then I'll understand your worth," Heather teased.

The day continued just as it had begun. People milled from room to room, their hands and mouths filled with food and their laughter boisterous. Nicole, Heather, and Casey flung themselves into the last preparations of the Thanksgiving meal. Finally, she pulled the turkey out of the oven around noon to allow it to cool for approximately forty minutes before serving. During this time, Kristine and Bella argued about the appropriate way to set the dining room table while Melody and Donnie squabbled over what kind of music to play for the dinner itself.

"Is our family crazy or what?" Heather said with a laugh as she analyzed a wine glass, lifting it high over her head before she scrubbed off a smudge with a towel.

"Maybe a little crazy, but still lovable," Luke said as he stepped in to collect several already-cleansed wine glasses to be set at the table.

"That's pretty sweet," Heather returned in a sing-song voice.

A knock rang out at the door, one that made Nicole nearly leap from her skin. She ran her fingers through her hair and then raced off to the front door, where she greeted Evan Snow and his (oftentimes very bratty) daughter, Maddy. Recently, during the festival they'd held to save the Keating Inn and Acadia Eatery, Maddy had run off with her boyfriend and stolen Luke's boat. Naturally, because she was a Snow, she hadn't been prosecuted, and Luke had been bright and easy about the whole thing, as was his way. Casey had heard him tell Heather once, *"Hey. I was a teenager once, you know. I was bad every now and then too"* At this, Heather reminded him, *"Luke. You were an orphan. Maddy has all the money in the world."* And Luke had responded sarcastically with, *"Oh right. Because money makes everyone happy and well-adjusted. That's right."*

Around one, Evan Snow carved the turkey in the kitchen as Nicole's eyes shimmered with excitement. Maddy texted, seemingly bored, in the corner. Heather flashed around and said, "I bet Grant's almost here! Should we wait a little bit longer?"

Casey's throat tightened with fear. The last thing she wanted was to admit her defeat in front of all these people, all at once.

"He said he got held up, darn it," Casey lamented with a sigh.

"When did he say that?" Melody asked.

"I just heard from him," Casey lied.

"When?" Melody demanded as her eyes turned to slits.

"About twenty minutes ago," Casey said.

"Why didn't you tell us?" Donnie demanded.

"Your mom's been slaving over the stove making the gravy for the mashed potatoes, that's why," Heather interjected, her words playful yet sharp with sassiness. "Now, everyone. Get to the dining room and take a seat. We've got Thanksgiving dinner to eat."

Casey cozied up between Melody and Nicole at the over-stuffed Thanksgiving dinner table. The table was laden with everything from fresh dinner rolls, turnip and mashed potatoes to homemade stuffing, turkey and gravy. Heather suggested that Luke say a prayer, which he did so with loving care, even as the feast before them steamed, emanating glorious spices and sinful smells of butter.

"I can't thank you enough, Oh Lord, for bringing us all together on this beautiful Thursday at the end of November," he said. "I've had a lifetime of loneliness and a sincere lack of family. Now, I find myself in the midst of one of the strangest..."

"Hey..." Heather warned playfully as they all remained with their eyes closed.

"Strangest, loving, hilarious, and beautiful families in the world," Luke corrected as both Kristine and Bella suppressed their laughter. "We thank you for these gifts, this love, and this food. Oh, Lord. Amen."

When they opened their eyes, Evan Snow remarked, "Not bad, Luke. Not bad."

Luke laughed outright. "It was my first try."

"Maybe you'll be better next year," Heather teased as Luke's eyes widened.

It seemed that a promise hovered between them: a promise that Luke would be a part of their family for years to come— a promise that Heather would love and adore him, for as long as he wanted to be there at the head of their table.

It was strange to see Heather fall for a man who wasn't Max Talbot— yet it was endearing to watch play out the beautiful texture of life and its malleability.

Chapter Five

L uke hovered in the center of the living room and stuck two fingers up. Casey, Abby, Nicole, Kristine, and Nate pulsed forward, hyper-focused, as Nicole called out, "Two words!" The opposite team sat with their arms crossed, watching the charade game with amusement. As it stood, the opposite team, with Heather, Bella, Donnie, Melody, Evan, and Maddy, was ahead by three points and no longer nervous about whether or not Luke grabbed this point. Casey felt out of her element and not like she contributed to her team. She had other things on her mind at the moment but continued to try to do her best anyway

Luke then insinuated that the two words made up a film title. Nicole clapped her hands together in excitement. "Genre! Give us the genre!"

At this, Luke dropped his shoulders back and made a kissy-face while Kristine howled, "Romance!" Luke pointed his finger at Kristine excitedly and nodded.

"A two-worded romance..." Abby muttered. "Are you kidding me? There are so many."

Casey glanced toward the opposite team, where she found Heather's dark blue eyes piercing her. She scowled strangely, and Casey had a hunch this had nothing at all to do with the game. Casey arched her brow toward Heather, who just mouthed, "Are you okay?" Casey rolled her eyes in response and returned her attention to Luke.

Luke was now on all fours. This seemed silly and unclear. He tore around down there for a moment while his team members yelled various ideas above him.

"Lion King?" This was Nate, who was maybe too intoxicated to catch the "romantic genre" thing.

Luke shook his head violently.

"Sweet Home, Alabama?" Abby tried.

Kristine arched an eyebrow toward her and said, "Two words, Abs."

"Oh, shoot. I just thought he was maybe a horse?" Abby returned.

"Where is the horse in *Sweet Home, Alabama?*" Kristine asked.

"Focus! We're losing time!" Nicole cried.

Luke then lifted his hands from the ground and formed what seemed like claws. Casey barked out, *"The Lobster?"* which was a terribly sorrowful but almost romantic movie she'd rented with Grant once around Valentine's Day— something she'd regretted renting, as it had seemingly pointed to the idiocy of looking for love in the first place.

Luke gestured toward Casey, excitement flashing across his face, as though she was on to something. Casey balked. She hadn't expected to get anywhere close to the answer. These had been her first words in at least an hour.

"So it's a lobster?" Casey asked tentatively.

Luke nodded as his eyes widened.

"Oh gosh. Um. What has a lobster in it?" Kristine demanded.

"*Mystic Pizza!*" Nate cried.

"I think that's mostly just pizza, Nate," Melody returned with a laugh.

"Hey. Stay on your own team!" Nate returned.

"Lobster. Lobster!" Nicole cried as she smashed her palm against her forehead.

"Mom. We won't be able to win if you have a concussion," Abby pointed out.

"Oh, I just got it," Kristine cried as she jumped to her feet. "It's *Annie Hall!*"

Luke popped up from the floor and howled, "That's it!"

Nicole shrieked and sprung to her feet to grip Kristine's hands and jump around. The edges of Casey's lips twisted upward. She slightly remembered the scene where Woody Allen's character and Annie Hall struggled through cooking a lobster meal, only for Woody to attempt the whole thing a bit later with another girlfriend. Was that all life was? An attempt to recreate what had come before?

"I don't know if that's a particularly romantic movie," Heather pointed out as they all settled down and grabbed more to drink. "Who wrote that one down?"

"I did," Bella admitted.

"I knew you were the one who wrote it," Kristine returned.

"Ah, look. Now I see why Kristine got it," Evan said playfully. "It's that twin thing."

"No! I got it because Casey understood Luke was a lobster," Kristine countered. "That was brilliant, Aunt Case."

Kristine gave Casey a genuine and beautiful smile. Casey tried to drum up some response about it, but her tongue felt as thick as sandpaper. In a flash, someone suggested that they have more slices of pie, that there was no such thing as too much pie on Thanksgiving. Someone else gave a resounding, "I agree!" and it was settled. Casey remained weighted on the couch.

She felt suddenly pulled into a memory of a different Thanksgiving.

It was the year Nicole had come to Bar Harbor and another year when she, Grant, Melody, and Donnie had flown out to Montana to meet up with Quintin, Henrietta, and Izzy, their last remaining daughter. At this time, Izzy had been twenty-six, and Frankie had been dead for two years after a horrible horseback riding accident. Izzy had been divorced and had a toddler, aged four. It had been strange to watch these gorgeous girls grow up and grow older, only to be marked with such tragedy and loss.

It had also been bizarre to sit within the dining room that Casey herself had designed at the age of twenty-two. She'd walked down the grand staircase and wandered through the hallways, genuinely amazed at her creative prowess from back then. At this time, age forty-four, the memory of her past self had felt like a dagger through her belly. She'd already betrayed her former being.

But also by this time, Grant had formulated himself as one of the top-selling businessmen in his field. Quintin, who'd grown into one heck of an alcoholic at this point, with a belly to boot, had greeted him warmly with, "I always knew you could do it, little brother." Grant had beamed at that, as though all his life, he'd just wanted praise from his older brother.

Casey had to wonder now: had Quintin belittled Grant for being a stay-at-home dad for all those years? Had Quintin pointed out that Casey had been the "more successful" one of the two of them? Had that possibly been the first crack in their marriage?

Suddenly, Heather sidled up against Casey on the couch. There was the clink and clang of countless spoons and forks in the next room as the others tore into pie and ice cream.

"It's almost like they'll go hungry or something," Heather said playfully, even as her eyes grew shadowed.

"They very well might," Casey countered as she shifted away from her youngest sister. Heather was the emotional one, the one more in-tune with her heart and her ever-billowing "feelings." Casey had never been that way. She almost regretted to say that, in many ways, she felt that sort of thinking was foolish. It sold Heather's books, though, that was for sure. But that's all it was really good for.

Silence brewed between them. Nate suggested that they soon do another round of karaoke in the kitchen, which Maddy Snow was "totally up for." Some of the cousins whooped while others groaned. It would be another long night at the Keating House.

"What's up with you?" Heather finally breathed. "You've hardly talked all day. And Nicole said she found you at the kitchen table at five-forty-five with a half-drunk pot of coffee."

"I couldn't sleep," Casey replied firmly.

"Yeah?" Heather sucked her cheeks in. "I've probably told you how little I slept after Max..." She closed her eyes tightly as emotion took hold of her.

Here we go, Casey thought now. In a way, she was grateful. Heather could take all the energy of this pain and put it squarely upon her shoulders. Casey wouldn't have to fess up to her true feelings. She would remain in peace.

But now, Heather's eyes snapped open once more. "You've been pretty cagey about Grant the past few months. I know that I've been in my head about a lot of my own stuff, but I'm here for you, Casey. I hope you know that. Whatever you're going through, whatever you want to say. You can trust me. I'm here for you. Okay?"

Casey placed her hand near her throat, surprised at Heather's articulate and nurturing way. She'd expected her to fall into tearful words. Instead, she found a powerful woman before her— a woman who'd dove into the depths of despair and come out stronger than ever.

"Thank you, Heather," Casey murmured. "I appreciate that."

The others returned to the living room for a round of twenty questions, which Casey forced herself to pay attention to. The large grandfather clock told her it was now five-thirty, yet both of her children seemed too caught up in the chaos of Thanksgiving to ask her again where their father was. He'd probably been gone so much the previous few years that it seemed second nature to them to count him out— what a funny thing. The four of them had been thick as thieves. Casey could have sworn it would last forever.

Perhaps Aunt Tracy would have said the same about the four of them— Tracy, Casey, Nicole, and Heather.

The night continued on. At various times, Casey found herself in conversation with Maddy, who informed her about her recent selection of paintings, all of the dreadful variety, or Nate, who made a hilarious impression of Will Ferrell that almost made Heather pee her pants. Abby appeared soon after, a little bit too drunk to speak properly, even as she tried desperately to articulate just how grateful she was for Casey giving her a place to crash after she lost her job in Providence. "You don't know how dark those days were for me, Aunt Casey," Abby explained as her eyes glittered. "I thought I was so screwed."

Casey longed to tell the poor girl how much she had felt that Abby saved her from the anxious, stirring thoughts of her own lonely soul. But it felt too vulnerable, especially in front of so many other people. So she just placed her hand over Abby's and said, "I'm just so happy we're all together now. Bar Harbor is a dream."

Around nine, Nicole forced everyone to sit in front of the television for another viewing of *Planes, Trains, and Automobiles*, which was their Aunt Tracy's favorite film. As Nicole settled in on the couch beside Casey, she whispered, "I just want to feel like she's here with us. I don't even know if that makes sense."

Melody cozied in beside Casey on the couch and folded her legs beneath her. Heather hustled in with a big bowl of frosted Christmas cookies, which Nicole scolded her about. "Are those store-bought?"

"Guilty. I just thought, you know, good little snacks for tonight?" Heather tried.

Nicole rolled her eyes as Nate and Donnie popped up to grab two each. Melody cried, "Hey! Pass me one!" And soon, nearly all the cut-out frosted Christmas treats were eaten.

As the first of the movie's soundtrack rolled over them, Melody lifted her chin toward Casey's ear and whispered, "I tried to text Dad earlier, but I noticed the text didn't go through?"

Casey's heart nearly stopped. "I'm sure he was just in the air, honey."

"I don't know. When was dad's plane supposed to land?"

"Shhh," Nicole murmured. She'd needed everyone to focus on the task at hand.

"We can talk later," Casey murmured to her daughter.

Casey had never given less attention to a film, not even the silly movies her children had asked to watch around the age of three or four, the ones that taught you to count or spell your name. As John Candy and Steve Martin whisked their way cross-country to try to reach Sweet Home, Chicago, in time for Thanksgiving, Casey wracked her brain for some sign in her life with Grant, anything that clued her into what Stacy's words had alluded to.

Did Grant have a secret life somewhere else that Casey wasn't aware of?

Was he perhaps having an affair with Stacy herself?

The thought curled through her mind and threatened to poison her. She closed her eyes as Nicole howled with laughter beside her in such a way that made the couch shake.

Somehow, against science itself, Casey fell asleep during the film. Perhaps this was due to her lack of rest the previous night; perhaps it was due to all the stress. It was difficult to say. When she blinked her eyes open, she found herself witnessing Luke and Evan in the midst of a conversation about the roads in downtown Bar Harbor and how someone really needed to fix the potholes. Men always resorted to conversations like this, didn't they? It was their comfort zone.

Nate was distracted in the corner with his cell phone. Melody read a fashion and art magazine, presumably for a better idea of what to sell next. Casey stood and wandered toward the kitchen, where she found Nicole, Heather, Kristine, and Bella at the kitchen table with mugs of coffee, gossiping about Bella's recent on-and-off boyfriend. If Casey closed her eyes and shifted her mind just so, she could half-imagine that Nicole and Heather were actually the same age as Kristine and Bella. It wasn't really long ago — was it?

"There she is. Our sleepy lady," Kristine teased.

"Ha," Casey returned.

"You needed it. You said you couldn't sleep last night," Heather countered.

"Yes. Not exactly my plan to sleep in front of everyone on Thanksgiving, but..."

"It happens to the best of us," Nicole replied. "Abby still won't let me forget how I did that in front of Michael's family about ten years ago. It was embarrassing for everyone. Right smack dab in the middle of the carpet." Nicole now shivered with laughter, even though the memory was probably very painful for her. "I am so grateful I never have to see that family again."

"What about Abby and Nate's weddings?" Kristine asked.

Nicole's eyes flashed. "We'll cross that bridge when we come to it."

"With Evan Snow on your arm, I have a hunch you'll win whatever war that is," Heather pointed out.

Nicole's lips twisted. "I don't know what you're talking about..."

Evan Snow appeared in the doorway and peered down at Nicole lovingly as though he'd sensed his name. "Maddy's informed me it's about time for us to go."

Nicole's face paled. "Oh shoot. That's too bad."

"I could come back after I drop her off..." Evan tried.

"Oh. Would you?" Nicole asked brightly as she popped up.

"Sure." Evan had no eyes for anyone else in the kitchen.

Casey, Heather, Kristine, and Bella exchanged humorous glances as Evan gave Nicole a firm nod and then stepped back. "I'll see you later, then," he said before he walked away.

The women in the kitchen held the silence for a long moment until they heard the click of the front door as it closed behind Evan and his daughter. On cue, Casey and Heather burst into laughter as Kristine imitated Evan. "I'll see you later, then," she mimicked in a sing-song voice.

"Gosh, you guys..." Nicole's blush was crimson. She fled the room as the others cackled.

Nate couldn't get the others in on Thanksgiving Karaoke despite his best efforts, as everyone felt too exhausted to sing cheesy songs into a makeshift microphone. Donnie flicked through the channels as night drifted toward midnight. Before long, many in their group made little excuses and fled up the stairs to sleep. Soon, even Donnie, Melody, and Nate were slumped in their designated living room sleeping areas— and only Casey remained awake, refreshed from her earlier nap on the couch.

Just as she turned for the staircase, there was a light knock at the door. Surprised, yet not wanting to wake the others, Casey hustled for the door and peered out to check on the late-night visitor.

The man who stood on the porch was familiar, all right.

Her heartbeat quickened as her mouth grew dry. Unable to breathe, she slowly drew the door open to find him before her— the man who, so long ago, she'd pledged her life to. The man she had known to be the love of her life.

"Grant. Hello."

Chapter Six

C asey hadn't seen Grant in the flesh in many months. Here he stood— all six foot three of him, his shoulders broad, with those sterling blue eyes and that handsome, crooked smile. He held a large bouquet of autumn flowers in his hands, edged with sunflowers. Everything about this moment seemed perfect, save for one thing.

Grant had a black eye.

Casey placed a hand over her heart as she gaped at him. Maine weather, ever a finicky thing, had kicked up a snowstorm, and big dollops of snow flattened themselves across his cheeks and forehead as the wind rushed up off Frenchman Bay. His black eye was particularly dark, proof that whoever had swung at him had really wanted to hurt him.

Was this part of the "secret" the secretary, Stacy, had insinuated?

"Hi," Grant rasped, his voice gruff but timid.

Casey had no words. She stumbled back and pressed a finger

against her lips before gesturing over toward the sleeping bodies of Donnie, Melody, and Nate. Grant tip-toed in with the flowers at his side. He closed the door against the rush of the wind and followed Casey into the kitchen. There, she closed the kitchen door. She slapped a hand on the counter as her rage that had bubbled for days within her sprung to the surface.

"What the hell, Grant?" She held her voice to only a whisper. It was laced with frustration and anger.

Grant's lips parted with shock. He placed the bouquet next to the stovetop and pressed his palms together. Casey felt like a person at one of his stupid business presentations. She didn't want to be sold anything she didn't need.

"You've had your phone off all day. You didn't answer me last night, nor did you call me back. You told me multiple times you'd be here for Thanksgiving, and I passed along that information to your children."

Grant's cheeks flushed, which contrasted his black eye strangely. He glanced toward the bay window as though someone over there might have an appropriate answer for him. Unfortunately for him, it was just the two of them: husband and wife, finally facing off.

She took a step closer to him. "And this black eye? What the hell, Grant?"

Grant placed a hand over his cheek as he sighed heavily. "I haven't had the chance to look at it all day. I've been traveling for hours to try to get here in time."

"In time? In time for what, Grant?" Casey gestured around the kitchen, with its half-eaten apple pie on the counter and its scattering of dirty forks in the sink. "We ate dinner at one. We always eat dinner at one. I don't know if you've paid attention to the past, oh, twenty-five years of Thanksgiving? But that's been the way Thanksgiving rolls from the way I remember it."

Grant gaped at her as his shoulders sagged. "I know, Casey. I get it. All I wanted was to be here today."

Casey could hardly believe her ears. "Then you should have been here yesterday or the day before yesterday. Most of the family arrived on Saturday, Grant. We've had non-stop family activities since then, all without you. And you know what? Until right now, all I wanted was for you to be here with me and your children. I wanted you to be here and remind me that everything will always be all right between us. But you know what I figured out today, Grant? I figured out that nothing is okay. Nothing's even a little bit okay between us. And the sooner I accept that the sooner I can move on to the next phase of my life."

Grant's lips parted in shock at her words. Casey relished this, albeit slightly, as her heart felt so bruised. The only thing she could think of was to hurt the person who'd hurt her so much, even though she knew how childish it was.

"Please, Casey. Don't you think you owe me at least a few minutes to explain?" Grant pleaded softly.

Casey's heart hammered in her chest. She shook her head almost violently, making her dark hair waft around her ears. "I can't, Grant. I can't take it. I can't take another night alone, just hoping you'll come back. I need some peace. And I've found it here in Bar Harbor with my sisters. We've built a whole world for ourselves here, out of the wreckage that our father left for us."

"What are you talking about?" Grant demanded.

Casey might have laughed had she had the strength. Within this conversation, she realized everything she hadn't told Grant about the past few months. There was only so much you could translate over phone and text. The crater between them was as large as the Grand Canyon. "Communication difficulties" hardly covered it. It was now as though they spoke different languages.

"I think it's about time we looked into divorce lawyers," Casey said firmly.

Grant's jaw dropped. He stumbled back toward the kitchen door as the air around them tightened. He shook his head ever-so-slightly. "You can't be serious, Casey. You're just angry."

If there was ever a wrong time to tell Casey Harvey that she was "just angry," it was this time. Casey pointed a firm finger toward the door and said, "I need you out of this house this instant, Grant. I want to work exclusively through lawyers from here on out. I suppose that shouldn't be so difficult for you since you find it pretty damn difficult to call me even every few days."

"I have so much to say, Casey... So much."

"Tell your lawyer," Casey boomed. "And get the hell off our property."

Slowly, Grant walked through the kitchen door and made his way down the hallway and back into the snow-filled night. Casey remained in the kitchen with her arms crossed over her chest as whatever car he'd brought revved its engine in the driveway. A moment later, Donnie, Grant's son, appeared in the kitchen to retrieve a glass of water. It was like seeing Grant's ghost. He yawned and said, "Did you hear something outside?"

Casey said she hadn't. She told him to go back to sleep.

"Only if you do, Mom. You look tired," Donnie told her.

"Didn't anyone ever tell you never to say that to a woman?" Casey remarked sharply.

Donnie sipped his water and grumbled sleepily. In another moment, he disappeared back into the hallway and allowed Casey to stew in her anger and her shame. How foolish she'd been to ever fall in love with that ruffian cowboy from Montana. She'd always assumed herself to be more intelligent than that, with none of the quivering emotion of her other sisters.

Now, she saw herself for what she truly was: here in Bar Harbor, jobless and soon-to-be-divorced. She felt like her world had just fallen apart. She collapsed at the kitchen table and bent her spine so that her forehead plastered itself across the shine of the table. That night, Bar Harbor would take on nine inches of snow within only two hours. But that's the thing about snowfall: it's quiet, unnoticeable until the sun splays across it and illuminates its glory.

Chapter Seven

A flickering light for a twenty-four-hour hotel in downtown Bar Harbor beckoned Grant Griffin as he eased his car through the impenetrable snowfall of late November. Under this shimmering snowfall, Bar Harbor looked picture-perfect, like a miniature village beneath the orb of a snow globe. This late at night on Thanksgiving, the streets ached with emptiness; cars parked on either side of Main Street took on the heaviness of many inches of snow already and, being Maine vehicles, prepared for still more before the morning light.

Grant had never been to Bar Harbor, despite his suggestion that he and Casey take the kids there for a hike through Acadia National Park, whenever that had been. Fifteen years ago? Maybe more? Regardless, Casey had scoffed at the idea and pointed out that she and her sisters had made a forever-pact never to darken a single Bar Harbor doorway. *"It's my father's territory. You know how I feel about Adam Keating."* Times had changed; the temperature had shifted. Grant felt like a man who'd stepped onto a movie set, armed with a script for a very different film. The woman who'd just sent him to the door with the threat of divorce had very much looked like the vibrant, gorgeous creature he'd committed his life to twenty-four years ago. To hear a voice that ached with such nostalgia and love for him, then to toss him out like yesterday's garbage— it nearly sliced him in two.

The downtown hotel seemed not to have a name. It was located within a large colonial house, seemingly transported from a long-ago family home to a creaky, nearly-haunted locale that accepted weary travelers just passing through. Grant couldn't envision anyone stopping here with their children for vacation. Even still, as he stepped through the front door, the receptionist greeted him warmly, with a droopy-eyed smile and a slow-worded, "Hello. Welcome to Bar Harbor."

Grant paid for a single room for one night. "Do you think that room will remain available over the weekend?"

The receptionist, a middle-aged man who wore a nametag that read, "Tyler," wore a golden band around his ring finger. The fat of his finger bulged out around it. Grant wondered if Tyler's wife detested his late hours at the hotel. Perhaps she liked having the bed to herself, if only a little bit.

"Oh, sure. It's not tourist season around here, as you can tell," Tyler pointed out. "We don't get many guests here at the hotel." He leaned down as his voice grew oddly sinister. "If you ask me, they should close this place down from November to March. But don't tell my superiors that. I need this job."

Grant told him he wouldn't tell. This seemed to please Tyler, who passed him his room key, a heavy, antique thing and informed him that his room was on the second floor.

"There's a bar in the back," Tyler said as Grant grabbed his

CHRISTMAS IN BAR HARBOR

suitcase. "We don't close up till three in the morning if you'd like a nightcap."

He could certainly use a nightcap or two, considering what just happened. Perhaps Tyler sensed this in Grant's face.

Well, the black eye was certainly a dead giveaway.

Grant headed up the creaky staircase to drop his suitcase off in room 27. The room offered a single queen-sized bed with four posters, an antique nightstand, and what looked to be a Walmart-brand wardrobe, which was a funny contrast to the other old-world artifacts within the room. There was a reason the place was cheap and empty. Its commitment to detail seemed inarticulate, at best.

The bar was located in the back room of the old colonial. It featured a wrap-around mahogany bar, with a plaque that explained that it had been taken directly from an old bar that had been quite famous during Bar Harbor's epic whaling days, the likes of which the little village hadn't seen in over one hundred years. The man behind the counter was perhaps forty, forty-one, with a clean-shaven face and a little bowtie. Grant imagined he detested the bowtie— that he'd toiled over the tie-up of it every day of his career at the hotel bar. The bartender churned a towel around and around the edge of a beer glass as he greeted Grant.

"Hey there. Happy Thanksgiving."

Grant slid upon a stool and nodded. He could feel the bartender zero in on his black eye; he could further feel the bartender's hesitation about bringing it up. He seemed to think better of it.

"What can I get for you?"

Grant ordered a whiskey neat, as was his recent custom after multiple business trips all over the world. People respected you

65

when you drank your whiskey neat, and respect was something he required in the world of sales. Most people these days looked at him with the modicum of respect he'd felt he always deserved; most people, that is, except his wife, who looked at him with a mix of sorrow lined with furious anger.

When the bartender placed the whiskey upon the counter, another man entered the bar. The bartender's smile cracked open.

"Hey there. I didn't expect you tonight."

The handsome stranger brought a hand forward to shake the bartender's warmly. "I brought you a slice of pie."

"You shouldn't have," the bartender returned.

"I knew you were stuck here all night. Doesn't seem right on a holiday like today."

"I might have to stay the night, too," the bartender continued. "That snow out there seems colossal."

"It isn't letting up; I'll tell you that," the stranger returned. He glanced over toward Grant and nodded firmly before ordering himself a whiskey, as well.

"It's whiskey night here at the hotel, I see," the bartender joked.

The stranger sat three stools away from Grant as the bartender poured his drink with the firm flick of his wrist.

"I don't know that I could put a beer in my belly after all that eating," the stranger continued.

His accent was strange, Grant realized now. He'd done enough traveling over the years to place accents rather well. This one? It seemed oddly Midwestern, with strange little pockets of outlier accents, as though he mixed and matched where he'd lived before this.

"You're in good with those Harvey sisters," the bartender remarked. "They won't let you get away without a full belly."

"My belt has gone up a notch. I'll tell you that," the stranger said with a boisterous laugh.

Grant's heart seized with sudden alarm. He sucked down too much whiskey as he contemplated what to do next. This stranger knew the "Harvey Sisters," seemingly so well that he'd been invited to Thanksgiving Dinner. Was it possible that Casey had some sort of romantic affair? Oh, but no. That was ridiculous. She'd tried to reach him the previous evening, waiting around for him all day, but he'd been occupied. Plus, Casey wasn't the sort to cheat.

Was she?

Or perhaps he now just projected other situations upon her.

How well could you ever really know someone?

"They had seven pies," the stranger continued. "I swear that we ate from one in the afternoon until eleven at night. It was like some kind of contest. After being shuffled from foster homes and orphanages, I tell you what, that was the Thanksgiving Dinner I always dreamed about."

The bartender laughed appreciatively. "If there's anyone who deserves it, it's you, Luke."

Luke. Grant had never heard the name before. He shifted strangely atop his stool so that it creaked beneath him. The bartender asked if he wanted another whiskey, and Grant requested a double.

"I've got to say," Luke, the stranger, began then. "Didn't expect to see anyone here at the hotel so late at night." His gaze flicked toward Grant with curiosity.

Perhaps this was the sort of town where you just talked to whoever sat at the bar with you. Grant wasn't entirely sure he was up for such banter. He could hardly be honest with his wife. He could hardly be honest with himself.

"I got caught in the storm," Grant offered, words that weren't entirely a lie but weren't entirely the truth, either.

"You from Maine?" Luke asked.

"Not originally, but I've lived here the past twenty-four years. In Portland, though. Not Bar Harbor."

"Wow. Yeah. I'm not from here originally, either."

"I can hear it in your O's," Grant said, accidentally smiling.

"Ah right. Midwestern, through and through. Guess I can't ever shake it."

Grant lifted his new double whiskey toward Luke— a friend, apparently, of the Harvey Sisters, then cheered him. "To coming here from far, far away."

"And finding home," Luke affirmed before he drank the rest of his whiskey and ordered another.

"Your Thanksgiving sounds a lot better than mine," Grant offered, surprising himself.

Luke arched an eyebrow as the bartender poured him another drink. "It all came as a surprise for me. I started working at the Keating Inn and Acadia Eatery a few years back. Maybe you've heard of it?"

Grant admitted that he had, without telling Luke, that Casey had demonized the inn as *a place she wouldn't go if it was the last place on earth.*

"I developed a close relationship with a man named Joseph Keating. An incredible human being. The kind of father I always dreamed of."

Joseph Keating? Casey's Uncle Joe? Grant stitched his brows together as Luke highlighted this strange, alternate reality. As far as

Grant knew, Joe Keating had been Adam Keating's right-hand man, another key figure in Adam's abandonment and the downfall of Jane Harvey.

"He and his brother passed along the Keating Inn and Acadia Eatery to his brother's daughters. He always thought there were three of them," Luke said as his eyes shimmered with excitement.

"Not so!" The bartender piped up from the far end of the bar as he continued to cleanse more beer glasses. Grant wondered who'd drunk from those glasses. It seemed unlikely that anyone had entered the shadowed doors of this hotel bar throughout Thanksgiving Day. Perhaps this was his way of killing time. Perhaps the bar itself was haunted— like something out of *The Shining*, and Grant would awaken to learn that Luke and the bartender had died seventy-five years before.

"Not so?" Grant echoed as his heart pulsed with intrigue. "What do you mean?"

"Ah, you're not from around here. What do you care?" Luke continued.

"I don't. Just need a bit of gossip to put me to sleep," Grant offered.

"They came back one by one," Luke went on. "Nicole first, then Heather and then Casey."

Grant inhaled sharply at the way Luke said Casey's name. It was so familiar to him, as though he'd said it thousands of times. How could this man look Grant in the eye and say his wife's name without knowing who he was? Grant felt like a traveler from another dimension.

"They've all been through so much heartache," Luke said. "The gamut, really."

"Divorce. Death. You name it, they've been through it," the

bartender affirmed, as though he was a know-it-all on the history of the Harvey Sisters.

"Heather... she lost her husband in a truly tragic way last year," Luke said.

Grant's heart darkened at the memory. Before his death, Max had been a spectacular person and one of Grant's greatest friends. When Grant had been a stay-at-home father throughout Casey's prosperous years in architecture, Max had been the first number Grant had called for assistance or just someone to talk to. It was tough to stay at home with two young children, a fact that made Grant frequently spout to colleagues and friends across the continent that "stay-at-home moms and dads deserve a full-time wage and a medal." Back then, Max and Heather had Kristine and Bella to raise— and several gut-bustlingly hilarious and head-scratching stories about raising twins. Often, Grant and Max had had late-night conversations while the children slept on.

"And I think she just wanted to look for answers about her past," Luke continued. "Boy, did she find answers."

The bartender whistled, impressed. There was a strange thudding sound between Grant's ears. Whatever this story was, it was big, and Casey had avoided telling it to him altogether.

"Anyway, Adam Keating was never her father. Her mother had tricked him, taken all his money and most of his properties, and then ultimately left him with toddler Heather, whom he eventually passed off to Jane Harvey— Nicole and Casey's mother, because he could hardly care for himself," Luke continued as his eyes widened. He placed both his hands near his ears and exploded them out like fireworks. "The Harvey Sisters could hardly believe it. It was like the world they'd once known no longer existed."

"Gosh..." Grant pressed his hands across his cheeks. The edge of his first finger ebbed against his black eye and a jolt of pain permeated up and down his face.

How had Casey kept all this from him? Why hadn't she at least mentioned this during one of their many phone calls, that Heather's parents weren't Jane and Adam? Sure, their phone calls had become briefer and quieter over the past few months. But Grant had thought that Casey would have verbalized it if something truly pressing had come up.

This was hypocrisy. He knew that. He'd been incredibly silent about a number of things.

Even still, this was proof of another crack within their relationship.

"You look white as a sheet," Luke noted now, incredulous.

Grant guffawed. "Sorry. Didn't get enough to eat today, I guess."

"You're just about the only person in Bar Harbor who feels that way, I reckon," Luke said. "You want a slice of pie?"

Grant sensed that a small forkful of Heather's apple pie would send him spiraling. It would take him to family reunions and Christmas celebrations and random birthday parties across multiple decades. It would stir within him a longing for a reality he could no longer return to.

"I've never seen someone grapple so much with whether or not he wants a slice of apple pie," Luke joked now.

Grant cleared his throat and tried his best to look distracted, as though he hadn't heard. The bartender and Luke exchanged looks that seemed to say, "Is this man a drunk, or what?" Grant's ego bruised slightly like the black ring around his eye.

"I guess I'd better use that bed I paid for upstairs," Grant grunted. He splayed a twenty across the counter and told the bartender to keep the change. As he made his way toward the doorway, Luke called out to him again.

"You never said where you were from— before Maine."

Grant clipped his hand around the edge of the doorway. After a long pause, he directed his eyes back toward Luke's.

"Further west than you," he said finally. "I had it in my mind I was a cowboy. Pretty stupid, huh?" He then disappeared into the shadows of the creaking hotel and ultimately collapsed in a heap on the mattress with the big scoop in the middle. It was a blessing that he did not dream.

Chapter Eight

In many years, the Keating Property hadn't seen such a thick blanket of early-winter snowfall. Sparkling droplets continued to shift from the grey skies above into mid-morning, beckoning the Harvey Sisters' children out into the waves of fluffy snow for wild snowball fights and attempts at snowmen. Heather joined and whipped one snowball after another toward her targets, Nate, Donnie, Abby, and Bella, as she howled with frantic joy and child-like energy. All bundled up on the front porch, Casey and Nicole sipped warm mugs of coffee and watched the glittering wonder-land-turned-war zone.

"I wish I had that energy," Nicole remarked with a laugh. "All I have is enough energy to chew this donut."

Casey nibbled at the outer edges of her maple-glazed donut and crossed her ankles. Each of them had donned two pairs of wool socks against the sharp-edged nature of this fresh winter's day. As Maine girls, they knew to lean heavily on the power of layered clothing, especially as the temperature dipped into the teens.

In fact, the teens were nothing for these Maine girls. Come February, the teens would feel like a balmy summer's day; such would be the contrast to the frigid days of high negatives. To be a Maine resident, you had to harden yourself to such realities. In a similar fashion, Casey supposed she had to harden herself to the reality of her approaching divorce. It would be a long, dark, wickedly cold winter— and she would spend each of those nights alone for the first time in twenty-four years. She would manage it the way she'd managed everything else.

"You're awful quiet this morning," Nicole pointed out as she took another bite of donut, one that resulted in chocolate cream bursting out of the center.

"I'm just tired," Casey replied.

"Did you get much sleep last night?"

"Not really," Casey admitted.

Nicole grumbled. "I wish I could give you advice about that. Meditation or yoga or acupuncture or…"

Casey shook her head as a strange swell of anger came over her. "I'm sure it's just stress."

"Has it helped to have the new project?" Nicole asked.

Casey arched her brow at Nicole; she sensed her facial expression was edged with disdain, yet didn't have the strength to calm it.

"I mean, for the new house. The blueprint you've been working on," Nicole offered hurriedly.

"Oh. Yes. I guess so." Casey sniffed, recognizing Nicole's pity. Casey wasn't the only one who noticed a sincere shift in her mood since her career had tanked. With Nicole's chef career off to the races and Heather's writing career skyrocketing, it seemed obvious they'd look at their successful sister and scratch their heads with confusion at the current events.

Casey wanted to tell Nicole to carve, "I used to be somebody," into Casey's gravestone. But she resisted the urge to go that dark. Not on the day after Thanksgiving.

Speaking of the day after Thanksgiving, it was, for better or for worse, Black Friday— a day that, traditionally, the Harvey Sisters spent together, shopping and gossiping and eventually grabbing dinner and a glass of wine. Heather burst back up to the porch to announce that it was nearly time for them to prepare for their multiple-hour shopping extravaganza. Casey longed to articulate just how little she wanted to wear her skinny jeans and join the world once again; Thanksgiving hadn't been particularly kind to her stomach. It sounded like borderline torture to stand in a dressing room and watch her body play out its middle-aged nature in the close mirror.

Well, there was that— along with the fact that she'd just told her husband she wanted a divorce after he'd appeared at the Keating House with a black eye. But she hadn't yet found the confidence to explain the situation to her sisters.

"Come on..." Heather nagged when she noted Casey's hesitancy. "We always do this. We can't break tradition, not this year of all years."

"You say that every year," Casey returned.

"Sue me," Heather returned as she walked up the steps and headed off to shower. "We're leaving in one hour!"

The cousins seemed relieved to have the Keating House to themselves for the day. As Nicole reversed the car out of the driveway, Bella, Nate, and Donnie all stood out on the front porch with enormous, mischievous grins on their faces. They waved their mittens to and fro in goodbye, assuredly making plans to play drinking games and blare music from Uncle Joe's stereo.

"I just hope they don't burn the place down," Nicole said with a sigh.

"We were so responsible at their age," Heather returned. "I was raising twin babies when I was Kristine and Bella's age."

"It's a different world," Nicole affirmed. "Guessing it'll be a little while before any of us reach the grandmother stage."

"Fine by me," Casey said, her voice flippant from the backseat.

Heather turned back to catch Casey's eye. "You don't want Melody and Donnie to enjoy the beautiful and nuanced experience of childrearing?" Her voice was heavy with sarcasm.

Casey rolled her eyes. "Of course, I want them to have kids if that's what they want. It's just... I know how confusing it was for Grant and me when I got pregnant by accident. Maybe we rushed into things. I don't want Melody or Donnie to have to rush into anything."

Heather and Nicole exchanged curious glances.

Casey scoffed. "Don't do that."

"Do what?" Nicole demanded.

"Don't have a whole conversation in the air about me without telling me what you're really thinking. It makes me spiral," Casey spat.

Heather's voice was quiet. "I just never knew that you regretted rushing things with Grant. You seemed so in love back then."

"You were younger than me. What did any of us know about anything?" Casey demanded, which shut them all up for the next fifteen minutes, as Nicole drove them into downtown Bar Harbor, where several cozy boutiques and bookstores lined the bustling streets.

Someone had already shoveled and salted the Bar Harbor sidewalks to allow for Black Friday shopping. Christmas garlands were strung from light post to light post; red ribbons fluttered with the icy breeze. Little stereos had been installed in various posts to allow for the slightest hint of Christmas cheer in the form of song. Even now, a tiny voice sang, "Silver Bells," shimmering in and out as they marched toward the first boutique.

Casey felt as though she'd walked through a Christmas nightmare. Everywhere they went, bright smiles created a direct contrast to the horrific and dark nature of her chaotic soul. Heather stretched a bright red sweater across her chest in the first boutique and gestured toward her sisters to ask, "Think I should try this on?" And the ease with which this conversation seemed to take form nearly made Casey burst into tears. She even heard herself say, "Oh, I don't know, Heather. Red has never really been your color," in a way that made her seem believable and very in the moment. Perhaps she could pretend to be normal like everyone else, even for the next few hours, before she collapsed yet again in her bed.

At the third boutique, Casey tried on a number of black dresses and modeled them to her sisters, who "oohed" and "aahed."

"Those legs!" Nicole hollered playfully as Casey strolled up and down the little hallway in the back of the store.

"She's killing it!" Heather cried.

Casey stopped short and analyzed the third of the little-black dress selection, tilting her hip to catch the line of her leg as it curved up toward her cinched-in waist. She was grateful not to see much of her Thanksgiving feast in this forgiving mirror.

A thought suddenly tore through her as she blinked at herself.

Should she buy this dress for the inevitable dates she would go on after the divorce went through?

Her knees clacked together as she staggered to the side of the hallway and inhaled sharply. She positioned her hands to the side of the wall and blinked at the ground as tears cascaded down her cheeks. There was no stopping them. She couldn't hold back her emotions any longer.

"Oh! Casey?" Heather scuttled forward with surprise.

"Casey, honey..." Nicole joined her on the other side.

Shrouded by the women she loved most in the world, Casey forced herself to breathe. She inhaled, exhaled, inhaled, and then exhaled. Slowly, the world pieced itself together before her again. Slowly, her thoughts took more articulate formation.

"What in the world just happened? What was that about?" Heather whispered.

"I have a granola bar in my purse. I want you to eat it," Nicole told her, concern laced across her face.

Casey shook her head. Nicole and Heather locked eyes yet again, displaying some sort of invisible conversation within the space. Casey's throat tightened. She couldn't bear this. Not a moment more.

"Grant arrived at the house last night," she breathed.

Heather's jaw dropped open. "You're kidding."

Casey shook her head despondently.

"What happened, honey?" Nicole whispered.

Casey sniffled. She felt utterly ridiculous in this two-hundred-dollar little black dress in the back of a boutique on Black Friday of all days. Sometimes, the truth picked its time to come to the surface. This was that time.

"I hadn't seen him in so long. We'd hardly talked. When I opened the door, he looked like a stranger. And on top of that..."

Could she really tell them this?

It was so embarrassing. It seemed the cherry on top of a moldy slice of pie.

"You can tell us, sweetie," Heather murmured.

"He had a black eye," Casey stuttered.

"Oh my god," Nicole breathed.

Casey clamped her eyes shut, willing this reality to fall away from her. Even in the silent darkness of herself, it remained the truth. How awful.

"Come on, honey. Let's get you out of this dress," Nicole suggested.

"There's a wine bar around the corner," Heather said firmly. "I'll go make sure we can grab a table as soon as possible." She walked off in her Louboutin heels, leaving Casey to sweep back into the dressing room and perform the embarrassing act of undressing herself beneath the horrific lights of the dressing room. They were like surgical lights.

Once at the wine bar with a glass of rosé in hand, Casey breathed easier. The space bustled with other women armed with shopping bags from recent Black Friday purchases. Different perfume fragrances wafted in the air around them. Upon Casey and Nicole's arrival, Heather had already purchased two bottles—a rosé and a Malbec as she waited for her sisters with three half-filled wine glasses.

Safe within the cocoon of their sisterly love, Casey found new ways to verbalize everything that had been going on for the past several years.

"I was so proud of him when he started his career," Casey breathed. "I knew it had been hard on him, in a way, to raise our children as a stay-at-home dad while my career flourished. I always wanted him to have his own thing. But then, he, of course, got one promotion after another until he spent at least a week, maybe more, out of the house per month. I missed him so much. He was my rock. Especially when it came to things like...." Casey paused as she tried to build the confidence to say it. "Especially when it came to my temper," she finally offered.

Nicole and Heather nodded knowingly. If there was anything Casey could be just then, it was honest. Being a sister meant going through one another's dirty laundry sometimes. Casey had been there just as much for Nicole and Heather— offering her home to Nicole after her marriage collapsed and being there every day for Heather after Max's disappearance.

It was her turn for support, she supposed. No matter how vulnerable that made her feel.

"I grew more and more volatile at work. I guess I've told you some of that," Casey continued. "I got into fights with colleagues I'd worked alongside for ten years or more. These fights really could have been avoided. It was just me, nit-picking, thinking I always knew best..."

Casey dropped her chin forward as a shiver coursed along her spine.

"But honestly, not having Grant around as often messed with me," Casey breathed. "He'd always been around. And then, one day, he went off and created a world all his own. Good for him, right? But he just kept claiming more and more of that world.

Even after I quit the architecture firm, his career skyrocketed. He told me it was time for him to bring in the money so that I could finally focus on the projects I wanted to do. But as you both know, I never got around to any of that. I'd lost my love for architecture while he'd found his true love, which is travel. In the past year, we've slept in the same bed no more than half the year."

Heather's lips formed a round O. Nicole shook her head despondently.

"Wednesday night, I called his secretary," Casey continued somberly. "Because Grant wasn't picking up his phone, and I just needed to know... know when he was coming, or if he was coming at all. His secretary was sleeping when I called her. Maybe she spoke out of line. I don't know. But what she told me, I'll never forget. She insinuated that there was a whole lot about Grant I would never know. And then, the very next day, Grant appears on the doorstep with flowers and a massive black eye."

Heather closed her eyes as a single tear trickled down her cheek. Casey could practically read her mind. She could practically feel the stories roll around the back of her head— stories that involved Grant as a vibrant young father of two, a man who'd befriended her husband, Max, in a way that had rivaled brotherly love. When Max had died, Grant had drunk himself into a stupor for five nights in a row before finally heading back out onto the road.

"What did you say about the black eye?" Nicole asked.

Casey buzzed her lips. "I told him that it was obvious our marriage was over."

"Casey!" Heather hissed.

Casey shrugged, suddenly flippant. She tossed back a huge gulp of her glass of rosé, yearning to forget.

"I want to do everything through lawyers," Casey affirmed. "I don't want to see his face again. It's too painful. And it's time for me to move on."

"Move on? From the love of your life?" Nicole demanded. "I think you may be jumping the gun here."

Casey arched an eyebrow. She longed to point out that Nicole had once thought Michael was the love of her life; how wrong she'd been about that monster. Perhaps Casey had been wrong, too.

"I just don't know about this, Casey. It seems rushed," Heather offered.

"The two of you haven't spent much time together over the past few years," Nicole said.

"That's so telling, isn't it?" Casey demanded. "He hasn't wanted to touch me with a ten-foot pole. Now, I've finally given him reason to leave for good."

Nicole and Heather gave one another side-long glances. This time, Casey didn't have the strength to nitpick them to death about it. She chugged the rest of her wine and filled her glass again as she riffled through the menu, on the hunt for small plates and tapas. She felt suddenly ravenous.

"Oh," she added suddenly, as her finger traced over the menu list of a fine selection of locally-sourced cheeses. "Nicole. If you could send me the name of your divorce lawyer, that would be fantastic. I want to get this started as soon as possible."

Chapter Nine

Sunday afternoon, Casey, Nicole, Heather, and Abby stood with heavy hearts as they bid goodbye to the rest of the vibrant, funny, and varied collection of cousins as they all headed off to their separate destinations. It had been a dynamic weekend of twenty-plus games of charades, a hundred (at least) songs of karaoke with the remote control used as the microphone, countless card games, and buckets and buckets of delightful food. Each agreed, in parting, that they couldn't wait for Christmas. It was mere weeks away, and it promised a host of more bright and beautiful stories, another few rounds of silly cousin spats, and gutbusting giggles.

Casey knew that by Christmas, her children would know about the divorce. Assuredly, their laughter wouldn't come as easily. She could only hope that they would comprehend the weight of Casey's decision and respect it.

Now, Melody flung her arms around Casey and placed her

chin delicately upon her shoulder. "I had such a great week with you, Mom," she breathed into her ear.

"I'm so flippin' proud of you, kiddo," Casey whispered in return. "Really, I don't know how you managed to build the career you have... but it's truly spectacular."

Melody stepped back slightly. Her ears were tinged bright red from the chill. "Dad texted me that he was sorry he missed Thanksgiving."

"He texted me, too." This was Donnie, who jumped up behind Melody and then swung around to hug Casey.

"He doesn't know what he missed," Melody lamented.

"I asked him what happened," Donnie tried. "He said his client list is just stacking up higher than he can deal with. I told him that means he owes you one heck of a Christmas present."

"Ha." Casey recognized the sarcasm within her single syllable and wished she could immediately take it back.

Her children eyed one another with curiosity and fear. Casey almost blurted out the truth just then. How difficult was it to tell your adult children, *"I'm divorcing your dad?"* It's not like they would throw their macaroni and cheese across the room (like Melody did once back in 2004) or mutilate their sister's doll (like Donnie did around the same time with a pair of scissors, perhaps as revenge for getting macaroni and cheese in his hair). They were grown adults. They would take it in stride. And, potentially, many years of therapy.

"We'll see you in a few weeks, Mom," Melody said with a hearty wave as she hustled down the porch steps and headed for her car. Donnie was hot on her heels. Long ago, Casey and Grant had burrowed themselves in bed and thanked their lucky stars that their children had such a close relationship with one another.

They would especially need that friendship now. It was the most powerful bond within their nuclear family.

Afterward, Heather drove Bella and Kristine to the airport while Melody and Donnie drove away. Nate leaped into his pickup truck and took off out into the wild winds, as well. This left only the foursome— the women who'd taken on the "burden" and joys of operating the Keating Inn and Acadia Eatery. The moment Nate's truck disappeared at the far edge of the curve in the road, Casey's shoulders shuddered forward. She had spent the previous few days in a state of pretending. Her body physically couldn't do it any longer.

"You okay?" Abby tried as Casey walked back into the house to fetch herself a glass of water. As she drank it down, she plotted the next hours and days of her life. That evening, she planned to operate the front desk at the Keating Inn as a way to pass the time — dealing with the silly intricacies of other people's lives. The following morning, she had a meeting with Bar Harbor-based divorce lawyer, Rachel Marris, who'd come highly recommended from Nicole's Portland-based divorce lawyer. "It's better to work with someone nearby," Nicole's lawyer had explained over the phone. "It's just more convenient if any papers have to be signed or if you have to come into the office and what not."

Rachel Marris was a high-powered divorce lawyer from Chicago who'd journeyed to Bar Harbor for "the love of what turned out to be a truly awful man." These were her words, delved out to Casey within the first two minutes of their meeting Monday morning at a local coffee shop, where Rachel liked to meet clients as she felt it was more comfortable than her current office. They sat in a private booth located at the back. She was five-foot-two with nearly white blonde hair and electric blue eyes.

Everything about her seemed angular, sharp, and somehow the direct antithesis of Bar Harbor.

"But my kids go to school here, and they love it," Rachel told her. "I wouldn't take them out and move them away. That would have been too much for them. I'm just a divorce lawyer. And guess what? People get divorced everywhere."

Casey soon learned that the majority of Rachel's clients lived in bigger cities across the Northeast, but Rachel was truly happy to take on a client right there in Bar Harbor. Rachel set herself up with her tablet and a portable keyboard so that she could take notes about Casey's particular case. Her eyes brightened as she said, "Okay, Casey. Tell me everything, and I mean, everything. Even small details could mean the world in your case."

Casey exhaled deeply. She'd only just managed to explain the full extent of her dirty laundry to her sisters. Now, this stranger appeared before her and wanted to do a deep dive into the intricacies of her twenty-four-year-old marriage. Was a twenty-four-year-old marriage a failure? They had outlasted most other divorced couples. Maybe that meant they had almost, kind of been a success?

"Well, my husband travels a great deal for work," Casey began tentatively.

Immediately, Rachel's fingers flung into action. This seemed ominous, as it didn't seem that Casey had provided enough information for all that Rachel now scribed.

"For years before that, he was our stay-at-home dad for the kids. My career was in high gear, and he liked being around for their big moments, you know? First words and first steps and all that. I felt like I was an awful mother to miss so much of that..."

Rachel continued to tap-tap-tap across the keyboard.

"Anyway, it became his turn to take charge of his career, which was fine with me. But then he started to spend too much time away. He took every opportunity. And in the past year, for example, we've only spent around... well." Her cheeks burned with embarrassment.

"Come on. I told you. No detail is too small," Rachel reminded her.

"Right. Well." Casey cleared her throat. "He's only maybe half the year at home, if that. He's been difficult to contact. And recently, in conversation with his secretary, I could sense that there's something... amiss."

"Amiss?" Rachel arched her eyebrow.

"Yes. Like, the secretary said there's a lot about Grant that I'll never fully know." Casey shuddered. "Gosh. That is not what you want to hear as the wife waiting around at home."

"No. I should say not," Rachel returned.

"The other night, he appeared in the middle of the night with a big black eye," Casey continued, basically whispering it. "It seemed to solidify what his secretary told me. That's when I told him to get the heck out."

Rachel nodded firmly. "And do you know where he went after that?"

"No idea. He drove off," Casey told her.

Rachel finished up a final round of typing before she removed her fingers from the keyboard and splayed them out across the gleaming wood of the coffee shop table. "I have to tell you, Casey, that I've seen cases like this before."

Casey's nostrils flared. "I see."

"There are many possible reasons for his seeming disappearance. Many possible forks in this road of story, but in this case, I smell a rat."

"I do, too," Casey breathed. "No matter how much I want to avoid the stench."

"Sometimes, these men have other lives. Sometimes, those other lives include other names, other wives, other children, and other bank accounts," Rachel continued.

Casey couldn't breathe. She stretched her hand over her throat as she willed the oxygen back into her lungs. Rachel's nodding seemed overwrought, as though she was a bobblehead toy.

"I know this is a lot to take in," Rachel said.

Casey leaned back against the seat. "You're telling me."

"But it's better to face the possibilities head-on so you can prepare for the worst later on," Rachel continued. "You have to trust me. As a divorce lawyer, I've seen it all—every nightmare scenario. Every doting husband gone wrong. It's why I have a series of check-ins that I do with every divorce, including checking in on any potential 'alternate reality' they might have built for themselves. Bank accounts that belong to him, even in another name, also belong to you. It's only fair that you know about them."

Casey nodded as a single tear rolled down her cheek. How was this happening?

"Thank you, Rachel. Really."

"Don't mention it."

"I really did have this sense when I saw him the other night that he was a stranger. That we'd never met before. That none of it had ever happened..."

"Casey, it did happen. It did. You had a wonderful life together. You had two beautiful children. I think it's better to honor what came before while still making plans for what comes next. Life is a story we tell ourselves and you're the main character."

Before she departed from the coffee shop, Casey ordered another cappuccino and sipped it on the half-mile walk back to the Keating Inn. Snow fluttered down around her as she stepped across the still-salted sidewalk. It seemed that the Christmas decor of Black Friday had been only the beginning, as on nearly every corner, more Bar Harbor residents took it upon themselves to add lights and tinsel and various Christmas scenes and trees. It was now November 29, and Bar Harbor was just as full-speed-ahead on Christmas as Casey was full-speed-ahead on divorce. It was a funny contrast.

Casey stepped through the double-wide doors of the Keating Inn foyer to find Abby in the midst of greeting a happy-looking yet frigid couple who reported they were from the "balmy south."

"We're far from home," the wife said as her teeth chattered together.

"But it's been her dream for years to come to Bar Harbor," the husband informed Abby as she checked them in. "Just hope we don't freeze here and have to stay forever!"

Abby chuckled good-naturedly. "You get used to it. And if not, well, I can recommend a wonderful winter coat store downtown. You might need more than those jackets."

"This is my thickest winter coat!" the wife cried.

"You told me it would be refreshing!" the husband offered, this time with the slightest hint of darkness.

Casey stepped around the front desk to join Abby as she typed the very-cold couple's details into the computer. Casey grinned at them warmly. Maybe she would never get married again. Maybe she would never be in any kind of marital dispute like this again. Maybe it was better that way.

"Good afternoon!" she greeted warmly. "Welcome to Bar Harbor. What plans do you two have while you're here?"

They chatted about the hikes they'd planned for, the breweries they wanted to visit, and the "relaxing hours in the upstairs library" they'd read about. Abby placed their heavy key on the counter and batted her long lashes as she wished them a "beautiful stay."

"And don't forget to check out the Acadia Eatery for lunch," Casey added. "My sister Nicole is the chef and the food is amazing, even though I'm biased."

"Ah! A family business," the wife returned brightly. "How nice."

The husband and wife team headed off toward their hotel room and left Casey and Abby at the front desk, with a glorious view of Frenchman Bay just beyond. Nicole and Heather popped out from the office to greet Casey warmly. Nicole's eyes were shadowed with expectation. Obviously, they'd all known where Casey had been that morning, including Abby, who they'd just clued in (making her promise not to tell Melody or Donnie yet).

"Well?" Nicole murmured.

Casey shrugged flippantly. Oh, how she wanted to be cheeky just then.

"I'm getting divorced," she said flatly. "The lawyer is going to do a full audit of his bank accounts, including ones that he may be hiding, along with any ties to anyone else in his life. She explained that it's a pretty common thing. Isn't that great? That something so awful could be so... freaking... common? Really. This is just so damn great."

Heather and Nicole exchanged glances.

"I just don't think Grant would do that to you," Heather breathed. "He's not like that."

"Heather. You're talking about a different version of Grant. You're talking about the version who shot hoops in the driveway with Max, Kristine, Bella, Donnie, and Melody. You're talking about the version of a man who perfected chocolate cupcakes and created a whole, elaborate scavenger hunt for Melody's thirteenth birthday. In marriage, you should be allowed to change. That Grant is dead. This is the one that remains."

The truth would rear its ugly head sooner than later, but Casey wasn't so sure if it was something she was ready to handle.

Chapter Ten

Grant Griffin hadn't yet found the strength to leave Bar Harbor. It was now the Tuesday after Thanksgiving and he'd sequestered himself to his little life at the untitled hotel downtown, adding on an extra night each morning to a very surprised receptionist, not Tyler, who said several times, "Are you sure you don't want to book a week straight? It's cheaper that way." But Grant Griffin felt as though he now lived on a planet without gravity, rhyme, or reason. How could he possibly know if he wanted to stay another night more until the sun rose again? Casey planned to leave him. All bets of time and space were off.

Tuesday morning, after he'd booked an additional night, he stepped out into the crisp Bar Harbor air and glanced down the road at his vehicle. On the front dash, there sat a large and crisp yellow slip sticking out of its envelope. His heart sank into his stomach. He rushed forward to find that, yep, he'd parked at the very edge of a no-parking zone— and the city official had written him a particularly heinous ticket. He cursed himself inwardly and then glanced down the road to find that the very official who'd probably given him this ticket remained on the road. In fact, she remained poised over another vehicle about fifty feet away, scribing yet another of her beautiful notes.

"Hey!" Grant rushed toward the older woman frantically with his yellow envelope lifted in the air.

She glanced toward him and gave him the most rueful look he'd ever received, even after twenty-four years of occasional arguments with the likes of Casey Harvey, the sassiest of them all. He stumbled forward, losing steam, and then happened to smack his foot against a patch of glassy ice. His foot flung forward as the rest of him fell back, and in a moment, his butt smashed against the hard sidewalk. A passer-by made an "Ooph" sound and winced as she marched past.

The meter lady took three steps toward him and curved her chin down to peer her cat-like eyes directly into his soul.

"Are you all right?" she finally asked, although there wasn't much in the way of pity in her words.

Grant was fine, just surprised and embarrassed. He flattened his hand across the sidewalk and pushed himself up. Once standing, he rubbed his hand across the bottom of his jeans in an attempt to get any ground stain off. He was a grown man with grown-up problems, yet this woman made him feel just about ten years old.

"I'm barely in the no-parking zone," he tried to reason with her.

The woman clucked her tongue. "Do you know how many times I hear that a day from tourists?"

"Oh, I'm not a tourist. Not really." Then what the heck was he?

"Well, you're not from around here. I know everyone around here," the woman told him.

Grant yearned to roll his eyes. He had traveled all over the world, met all sorts of people, yet there was something generally presumptuous about people from small towns. They were the ultimate know-it-alls.

"My wife just moved here," Grant returned suddenly, surprising himself. This was no longer about the parking ticket. This was about something bigger than that— about being known for his connection to Mount Desert Island. His wife was Casey Harvey, for goodness sake. And he loved her.

The woman arched an eyebrow then.

"You probably know her. She's Adam Keating's eldest daughter," Grant said.

"Well. I suppose I've met her a few times by now, sure." The woman's tone shifted, growing warmer. "And you know my favorite thing about Casey so far?"

"What's that?" Grant could have told her one million of his favorite things about Casey Harvey. He could have written sonnets about it.

"She's always parking in the appropriate parking zones," the woman told him pointedly before she turned around and sauntered back toward the vehicle she'd been on the verge of ticketing. Once there, she placed the windshield wiper over the brand-new yellow envelope with finality and force.

The woman was determined at her job, that was for sure. Grant had to give her that at least, despite the heaviness of the ticket in his hand.

Grant returned to his hotel room to field a work video call, which required very little input from him, thank goodness.

Frequently, as his boss rattled on about sales and what-not, Grant's eyes scanned the glow of the single pane window, which offered a postcard-perfect view of a downtown that exuded Christmas cheer.

"Griffin? You hear me?" His boss blared out through time and space to dig into Grant's depressed psyche.

"Loud and clear, Mr. Martin," Grant affirmed.

"We've got a number of sales to close out before the New Year, and dammit, I think we've got them in the bag with you as the face of the company," Mr. Martin continued. "I'm proud of all the hard work you've put in. You've put our little business on the map."

Perhaps six months ago, Grant might have taken this nugget of a compliment and celebrated. Now, however, he felt it like a stone in his belly. He waited for the end of the meeting before he smacked his laptop closed, donned his winter coat and thick winter hat, and then walked out back onto the sidewalk. It was four in the afternoon and it was already headed straight toward darkness, which was normal for a late November. It was sinister to count the hours of darkness you lived through as a Maine resident. It made the summer months all the more precious.

Grant's feet traced him back toward the Keating Property, where he stood to gaze up at that glorious white mansion on the hill overlooking Frenchman Bay. According to what he'd been able to discover online, this property had been the last dilapidated portion of Adam Keating's estate after his second wife, Melanie, had cleaned him out and left both him and her toddler behind. After Adam Keating's death, Joseph Keating had propelled the Keating Inn and Acadia Eatery to relative prominence, that is until

Nicole Harvey had tucked the property under her wing and shot it straight to the sky.

Since Nicole, Casey, and Heather's take-over, the Keating Inn and Acadia Eatery had been featured in a number of hospitality magazines, including *Maine Monthly*. Nicole was touted as the "chef to look out for on the east coast," while Casey and Heather were described as intricate parts of an ever-churning machine. In one interview, Heather called the Keating Inn a "beautiful setting for many of my future books," while Casey said it was a "perfect hideaway from real life."

Was the real-life she referred to the one she'd shared with Grant?

Grant forced himself up the porch steps and entered the gorgeous, old-world foyer of the colonial mansion, with its winding staircase, its deep mahogany walls, and it's beautiful hanging tapestry and antique paintings. It now seemed ridiculous that Casey and her sisters demonized this quaint place after all those decades— a place that their father had labeled for them in his will. It was like something out of an old illustration book, something you thanked your lucky stars you'd walked into.

Just as he'd prayed for, Casey stood on the opposite side of the front desk with a phone pressed against her ear and her long locks flowing lusciously down her shoulders and back. At this moment, she hadn't yet noticed him, which allowed Grant to take in the full breadth of her beauty, which had only deepened over time, as her face had lost its girlishness and become stoic, majestic, like queens in old paintings he'd witnessed when he'd gone to Europe for school as a teenager. She often said that she didn't have the beauty of her younger sister, Heather and that this had been commented upon throughout their high school years. Grant had never understood this sentiment. To him, Casey was the pinnacle.

Her dark eyes erupted through his reverie as they met his. Slowly, she removed the receiver from her ear and placed it delicately in the cradle. They stood off like this, like characters in a cowboy movie, as the rest of the hotel's life whirred around them. Two staff members walked between them, carrying an enormous Christmas tree and squabbling over who had the greater weight. A young woman stood at the top of a large ladder. She dusted the ceiling fan, which had assuredly hardly been in operation over the previous four months, at least, especially as they'd had a particularly chilly summer. All the while, Grant remained captivated by his beautiful wife.

To break the strange air between them, Heather burst out from the back office and cried, "Casey! You have to read this email." She stopped short, followed Casey's gaze, and gaped at Grant. He felt like a sideshow at a carnival.

"Hi, Heather," Grant said as he lifted a hand. He hadn't seen her in quite some time, maybe since early summer. Back then, she'd been a shadow of her former self. Casey had worried she would eventually have to drive her to a psychiatric clinic, as Heather resisted assistance from both Nicole and Casey at every turn.

Now, despite her current shock at his arrival, she looked vibrant, nourished. Perhaps Casey was right. The Harvey Sisters belonged in Bar Harbor.

"Hi Grant," Heather breathed.

Casey whipped around the counter, wearing a ridiculous smile, one that she'd seemingly created for show at the Keating

Inn. Hospitality wasn't exactly something Casey Harvey was made for. Grant had seen enough outbursts to know that well.

"What are you doing here?" Casey asked through a grit-teeth smile. She gripped his upper bicep and attempted to guide him toward the front door.

Unfortunately for Casey, Grant had never lost that strength he'd brewed up during long hours on the ranches of Montana. He held strong as a wall.

"I need to talk to you," Grant told her firmly.

"I thought you got the gist," Casey returned, still with that stupid fake grin. "I thought you left Bar Harbor days ago. And don't you have some business meeting or another to run off to? This is the longest you've stayed anywhere in months."

She was right; this was the longest he'd stayed anywhere. He was surprised at how much he appreciated the thickening roots beneath him.

"I can't just leave until we resolve this," Grant told her firmly.

"What is there to resolve? We've grown apart. It happens all the time. What's the statistic these days? Fifty percent? You'd have to be stupid to marry with those odds," Casey returned flippantly.

At the desk, Heather, who was an out-and-out romantic, winced.

"Come on, Casey. We have something special," Grant muttered.

Back in the Acadia Eatery, the two staff members with the Christmas tree attempted to prop it against the tallest wall, but as they swung it up, it immediately fell back to the ground with a wild crash. Several already-set dining room tables fell to the ground, shattering wine glasses in all directions. Several tourists in the hotel foyer shrieked as Heather shot back, grabbing a broom as she went.

"I've never seen Heather move that fast," Grant commented as Casey placed her hands on her cheeks in shock.

"I have to go," Casey blared. But before she did, she turned and gave Grant another of her horrific and terrifying gazes. "But I don't want to see you here again. This is my space, my family's space."

Grant opened his lips in preparation to tell her that he was her family, too. But before he could, she continued.

"Maybe it's best that I spell this out for you completely." Casey's nose twitched as she continued down this seemingly never-ending train of thought. "It's over. And if you have any respect for yourself and for what we had together, you'll take what I say as reality and leave."

Grant felt as though Casey had lifted one of the shards of a shattered wine glass and ripped it through his heart. He stepped back as the shock of the moment rippled between them.

"You should go," she said as he nodded back toward the dilapidated Christmas tree. He then forced himself around and hustled back into the sharp chill of the afternoon. Something in his pocket fluttered out, caught by the wind, and he hurried to catch it, only to discover that it was his parking ticket. Fantastic.

It had been quite a day.

Grant found himself back at the hotel bar, which now featured two other hotel guests, thank goodness. It took some of the pressure off of him and his rather reckless, lonely drinking. He didn't like feeling the penetrating eyes of the bartender.

"Hi Frank," he said to the bartender as he sat down.

"Another whiskey for you, Mr. Griffin?"

"Let's do a beer for now," Grant told him. Beer was something like dinner, wasn't it? He hadn't bothered with lunch, either.

"I keep thinking that I won't see you around here again," Frank continued. "The receptionist says that you only ever book for one night."

Grant could envision the staff members of the hotel hanging around, gossiping about "that strange man who won't leave." Probably it wouldn't be long now before everyone pinned him as Casey's rogue soon-to-be-ex-husband.

In fact, the look of curiosity mixed with pity that emanated from the bartender's eyes forced Grant back out onto the street after his first beer. It was a purple-skied dusk, and Frenchman Bay frothed gently beneath the first dots of stars. Over the previous few years, Grant had grown accustomed to sleeping in bed alone at night, but there was something about the frigid cold of Maine nights that made it far more difficult. He supposed this was especially related to the fact that Casey was just down the road and she wanted nothing to do with him.

When Casey had been five months pregnant with Melody, Grant and Casey purchased a large beautiful four-bedroom home in Portland with the aim to raise their family there. At the time, Grant had told Max that it mattered very little to him that Casey put up most of the funds for the house. Sharp pain in the base of his stomach had suggested a different kind of feeling— not one of jealousy, per se, but one of regret that he hadn't been allowed, yet, to reach whatever destiny his talents would have allowed. He wasn't delusional enough to think he could have "made it" as some kind of raucous cowboy. But he was good with his hands and good with people. Perhaps that could have counted for something.

However, the minute Grant held Melody in his arms, his simmering desire to be anything but a wonderful dad faded. He poured himself into that dynamic: offering tips to other mothers at the playground and priding himself on his ability to change a diaper in no time flat.

Once, his brother, Quintin, had come to Maine to meet his children. With Casey's hectic schedule, they hadn't yet had time to travel out to Montana, which had bruised Grant's heart. He'd wanted his children to have the best of both worlds— the rocky coastline and frothing seas of Maine and the great, wide-open skies of Montana. At least initially, he'd been grateful that Quintin had made the trek, as back then, he'd still been a very successful rancher with a grueling schedule of his own. Excitement to see his brother had faded quickly, however.

"What do you think your son will think of you if you don't make something of yourself?" Quintin had asked as he'd puffed a cigar on Grant's back porch.

The comment had needled him, although he'd initially brushed it off.

"Casey's a rock star," he'd told him. "It's not like I can just tell her to stay home when she has such a creative ability."

After all, Quintin had been the one to bring Casey to her level of architectural stardom. Shouldn't he have understood? Or was it just more important to him to belittle his little brother than to offer any excitement toward Casey's career?

Grant found himself along the edge of the docks, which were lined with dark green moss and creaked against the volatility of the incoming waves. He gripped one of the wooden poles and shuddered as an immense feeling of loss took hold of him. He was now forty-seven years old, and he had the career he'd always dreamed about. It was only now that he realized just how empty that was.

His phone buzzed with a call from the devil himself.

Grant answered it on the third ring.

"Grant? You there?" Quintin slurred his words together horribly. He sounded so far away. Grant could half-envision him outside of that dank saloon on the edge of the Montana town where they had grown up.

"I'm here," Grant answered begrudgingly.

There was silence for a moment, followed by a strange crash. Quintin coughed wildly, an indication that he'd recently smoked one of his disgusting cigars, leftovers from his long-ago days of wealth.

"How are you doing, Grant? Where are you at these days?"

Grant wanted to tell Quintin that they'd spoken as recently as the week before, but decided to hold it in. "I'm over in Maine, actually."

"Brr. You couldn't pay me enough to be there right now. Guessing you're frozen stiff."

Grant wanted to urge his brother to get to the point. These conversations always went the same direction, anyway.

"I hate to ask this of you, Grant. And you know I'll get it back to you. You know I will."

Grant's nostrils flared as anger welled up in his stomach. "How much do you need this time?"

Quintin coughed again. "You know I hate to ask."

Grant wanted to blare that there was a lot of proof that Quintin didn't hate asking for money. After all, he'd done it with moderate consistency the previous few years. With another rush of madness, Grant whipped around and said, "Dammit. I'll give you whatever you need, but this is the last time. And then, it's over. Do you hear me? It's really over."

Quintin fell into another flurry of coughs on the other end of the line. Grant's heart drummed wildly in his chest. At that moment, a gasp erupted behind him, and he turned to find none other than Luke, the guy from the bar, holding hands with Heather Harvey. It seemed they'd thought a little stroll near the docks was perfect for this time of night, too.

Heather's face was stricken with horror. Grant played out the last words he'd said— "It's over. Do you hear me? It's really over," and reasoned that probably, she'd gotten the wrong idea. His jaw dropped open as the two assessed one another. He quickly ended the call and dealt with the new problem at hand.

"Heather. It's not what you think..."

But Heather quickly walked back up the boardwalk as the snow fluttered around them. Luke's eyes widened as he followed after her. As she staggered back, Heather finally managed to find her words.

"You know what, Grant. I was on your side," she whispered. "I never imagined in a million years you could hurt Casey like that." She then turned around and hustled up the boardwalk, with Luke hot on her heels.

Grant remained as the snow flurried around him, a staggeringly lonely cowboy in the midst of the coldest winter on earth. He yearned for home, for his wife— yet knew it no longer existed. His home had been in Casey's arms.

Chapter Eleven

Nicole sat cross-legged atop Uncle Joe's old desk in the Keating Inn office with a large clipboard splayed across her thighs. Casey watched as she scribed out a list of "Christmas Specials" for the Acadia Eatery, including difficult and time-consuming recipes like soufflé, none of which she could be persuaded not to try.

"This is my first Christmas as head chef. I have to push my limits. I have to experiment," she'd told Heather and Casey.

Heather painted her nails in the corner, similarly cross-legged in a big cozy reading chair, which was positioned where a beam of light streamed in from a strangely beautiful, sunny winter day. Her phone sat beside her and offered a constant stream of conversation from Kristine and Bella, who spoke all at once to describe a recent Brooklyn-based party they'd attended, where they'd met a filmmaker woman who wanted to make Heather's books into movies.

It was a rather slow afternoon at the Keating Inn. Luke operated the lunch rush in the Eatery while the three Harvey Sisters sat comfortably in the office. Abby sat at the front desk and offered a bright smile of greeting to passers-by. It was December 3rd and the "Official Start of Christmas," in many respects, across Bar Harbor. The Keating Inn itself was busted to the gills with Christmas cheer, with a Christmas tree in nearly every room and tinsel sparkling in every corner. Casey had a hunch they'd be pulling tinsel out of every crevice of the place until July.

"I just don't know if the book would translate well to film," Heather articulated to her daughters thoughtfully as she waved a hand to dry her nails. "It's not that I'm not interested in a meeting. I just don't know..."

Kristine laughed wryly. "Mom. This is the game. You have to push yourself into that ring."

"Come on, Kris. If she doesn't want to, she doesn't want to," Bella returned.

"I'll take the meeting..." Heather offered again. "I just don't want a hack-it job when it comes to something so close to my heart."

Casey nabbed a Christmas-themed Reese's cup from a little bowl they'd set up for themselves in the office and unwrapped it distractedly. Heather told her girls she would call them later and then splayed her hands over her forehead. Nicole muttered inwardly about a selection of ingredients she would have to purchase for the upcoming Christmas menu.

"That sounds exciting," Casey tried, surprising herself at her ability to have any sort of conversation that didn't revolve around the very sincere wreckage of her heart and family.

Heather's nails caught the light as she whipped her hands back to her thighs. "Casey. I can't keep this in any longer."

Casey arched an eyebrow. "What's wrong?" Nothing good ever came from words like this.

Nicole lifted her head from her intense ingredient concentration.

"Luke and I went out for a walk the other night by the docks," Heather breathed. "Usually, it's pretty empty down there and just so wistful, you know. But as we got closer to the docks, we saw a man on the phone alone. He was really upset. Yelling about something, and when I got closer, I realized it was Grant."

Casey steadied herself against the wall. The Reese's cup continued to melt across her tongue. How was it possible he hadn't left town yet? Hadn't she been profoundly clear when he'd come into the Keating Inn the other day?

"It doesn't matter to me what he does in his spare time," Casey tried, although even as the words dropped from her tongue, she regretted them. Her sisters knew the intensity of her love for Grant; they knew better than to believe her.

"It's just... I have to tell you what he said," Heather said finally.

Nicole set down her pencil and dropped down from the desk, as though prepared for some kind of natural disaster. Casey forgot, for a long moment, to breathe.

"It sounded like he was breaking something off with someone," Heather stuttered. "He told whoever it was on the other end of the line that it was over. And I mean, it wasn't in a quiet tone either."

Casey's heart dropped into her stomach. Countless images entered her head, none of them wanted. She visualized Grant off somewhere around the globe— maybe California, Texas, or Florida, with a much younger girlfriend. She pictured them walking and talking, arm-in-arm, as the sun illuminated behind them. Perhaps the memory of his cozy world with Casey was something he could shove into the back of his skull for safekeeping while she wandered around their ghost-filled house alone.

"You don't know anything for sure," Nicole articulated now.

"Come on, Nicole. This coming from you?" Casey snapped.

Nicole dropped her chin to her chest. A heaviness filled the air between them as Casey fell into personal humiliation and shock. Michael had run off to build a whole other family. Was it possible that Grant planned to do the same? But then, this contradicted what Heather had heard. He'd ended it, whatever it was. But why?

"I'm just saying. You have no idea who he was on the phone with," Nicole countered. "And besides. Whatever it was, it's over."

"Yeah? So, you're saying I should just forgive and forget?" Casey demanded.

Nicole shrugged. "I just think you should give him the opportunity to talk to you."

"And what if you'd given Michael more chances to talk?"

"I did. He didn't want to," Nicole replied as her cheeks burned ruby red.

This shut Casey up for a moment. Nicole reached across the desk and flicked a tissue from its box before blowing her nose. Casey stewed with regret. It had always been clear to Heather and Casey that Michael had a consistent one-foot-out-the-door mentality. He hadn't thought twice about running out the door as fast as possible.

"This is just what men do, right?" Casey said softly. "Not to give them any kind of pass. But I mean, look at Dad. He set the blueprint for how everything else in our lives was supposed to go. I've hardly seen Grant over the past few years. He's a stranger to me. This phone call that Heather heard? It's an indication that I'm making the right choice. We had a beautiful couple of decades together. We really did and I am so grateful for them. What else could I possibly ask for?"

Nicole and Heather exchanged worried glances. Heather opened her lips to speak. But as the silence stretched on, there came the sound of a wild collection of what sounded like teenagers, giggling and gossiping as they entered the double-wide doors of the old Keating Inn mansion.

Casey stepped toward the doorway, watching the fifteen or sixteen teens lined up around the foyer, each dressed in wool coats and thick hats, many of which seemed to have been knitted by their mothers or grandmothers. A choir director lifted his baton and inhaled deeply, an act that led the rest of them to inhale on cue as well.

"Hark! The Harold angels sing, glory to the newborn king," the choir began, with the soprano singers surging on high and the baritone boys bellowing far below. The density of the singers' voices filled up the foyer and brought several Keating Inn guests down the staircase to enjoy the showcase.

Casey stepped up alongside Abby, who looked captivated. Her eyes glistened with excitement. Casey tried her darnedest to take in the brevity of this emotional moment. She tried to engage her ears with the lyrics, which should have brought on aching nostalgia and Christmas joy. She found none of that within her.

It's meant to be, she told herself then as the singers switched the pages of their songbooks and started on, "Have a Holly, Jolly Christmas," a song that seemed laughable in contrast to Casey's current emotional wellbeing (or lack thereof).

It's time to begin a fresh chapter— a Bar Harbor chapter. You can be whoever it is you've always dreamed of being.

But even as the thoughts formed in the back of her mind, she dismissed them. All she'd ever wanted was the life she'd had. It was now as though she stood above a blank piece of paper, prepared to draw out an architectural plan for a building she wanted nothing to do with. She just wanted her life back.

Chapter Twelve

Grant agreed to a very brief business trip to Seattle and departed Bar Harbor with a heavy heart that Saturday. He spent all of Sunday in his Seattle hotel room, plotting out the presentation he planned to give the following morning and tried his darnedest not to consider the weight of what he'd done. Had leaving Bar Harbor put the final nail in the coffin of his marriage? Or had he done that himself when Heather had caught him on the phone with Quintin?

At his sales presentations throughout that Monday, he was his same-old vibrant self, shaking hands and remembering small details about previous clients, down to, "How is your grandson doing at soccer these days?" and, "Now tell me. How are you feeling now that you've taken gluten out of your diet?" All the while, it was as though he dragged a shadow along behind him. When one of his previous clients asked after his wife and children, his smile nearly cracked his face open. "They're just fantastic, as ever. Melody's career is off to the races, and Casey's, well, she's just

a firecracker. The reason I fell in love with her in the first place."
He sounded like a madman, probably— a madman who would
never fall out of love with that brilliant young woman he'd met in
his brother's dining room. He'd never planned to.

Monday evening, armed with the confidence that came with a
number of sales, he sat down before his computer and researched
"best restaurants in Bar Harbor area." He then ordered a large
bouquet of roses (yet again) to have them ready by Wednesday
afternoon. He would be damned if he wouldn't fight for this
woman. He'd failed her in countless ways and, in the process, ultimately failed himself and their family. A pricey meal and a few
roses wouldn't cut it, but perhaps they would allow him a seat at
the table with her. Perhaps they would allow him a few syllables to
apologize.

With the expensive restaurant booked and the flowers paid for,
Grant then prepared himself for the most difficult task of all.

When Melody and Donnie had purchased the smartphone for
Grant's forty-second birthday, Grant had initially declared that it
was "useless." Now, the number of apps he used for messaging
alone was incomprehensible. All he wanted to do was reach out to
his wife. All he wanted to do was hold her.

**GRANT: Hi. I wanted to let you know. I'll be back in
Bar Harbor on Wednesday morning. I'd love to talk to you
in person. There's so much we haven't told one another.
Maybe we should give ourselves the chance to try.**

**GRANT: I'll be at the hotel downtown. I hope to see
you soon.**

Tuesday, Grant continued to take more sales meetings and
eyed his phone as though it was a bomb about to go off. His
passion took on a state of mania by the afternoon, one that

surprisingly brought even higher sales percentages than previously. His boss called him to lend a "Congratulations," while several of his colleagues emailed him to ask for his top secrets in the field. Grant longed to write back, "Just be fully devoted to your work twenty-four-seven and not your wife, and I guess you'll prosper at work." That was the sort of email that would get people talking, not in a good way. In the end, he didn't respond.

Wednesday at six in the morning, he took a flight from Seattle out to Maine, where he then grabbed his car and traced the unfamiliar route to Bar Harbor, the cozy colonial-looking New England village at the base of a mountain and the edge of a rocky coast. It seemed something straight from a calendar of paintings Quintin and Grant's mother had had hanging in their kitchen forty years before. She'd kept several of the calendars years after, all filled with her handwriting: QUINTIN - FOOTBALL PRACTICE. GRANT - HORSEBACK RIDING. QUINTIN - DRIVING TEST. That kind of thing. They'd thrown the calendars out after her death, something Grant regretted now. They'd been perfect snapshots of another time.

He'd tried to create similar calendars for his children during their earlier years as a way to link himself with his mother, but he'd been utterly unorganized when it came to things like time.

Back inside the hotel, the receptionist batted her false eyelashes at him with surprise. It seemed that Tyler worked nights and allowed this more judgmental receptionist the day shift.

"I never thought I'd see you again," she said, sounding bored.

"Can I have the same room?" He set his suitcase down beside himself and riffled for his wallet. "This time, I'd like to book a week."

"Really. A week? There's another surprise," the receptionist said as she clacked her nails over the keyboard of the computer and arranged his stay.

It was now Wednesday at three-thirty in the afternoon. Grant hadn't yet heard from Casey but still hoped that she'd respond to his text or call. Or that she'd even appear at the hotel, hungry to rip him a new one. Grant was willing to fight, as long as it meant he could see her. He wouldn't let her temper get the better of them both. It was a creature all its own. He'd heard her weep about it time and time again. *"I just can't control it when it takes over me. It's like I become someone else." "Casey, darling, you're the most caring and loving creature I've ever known. It's just that sometimes, you care and love too much. You can't help it,"* he'd told her in response.

Grant hung his suit on the outer hanger of the bathroom door in his upstairs bedroom, whistling an old Pink Floyd to himself. Outside, it seemed Bar Harbor residents had poured even more Christmas cheer over the streets. As though everything now was a fictional universe, a carriage whipped past, upon which a man dressed as Santa Claus directed the horses.

He couldn't wait to describe this to Casey later. He couldn't wait to tell her just how ridiculous yet glorious it was to live within the streets of Bar Harbor. "Maybe you're right. We should live here," he would tell her. On second thought, he would remove the "maybe" in that sentence. There wouldn't be any more "maybes" within the story of Grant and Casey.

At four-thirty, Grant sat at the edge of his bed and clicked through the TV channels before turning the thing off and listening to a podcast about self-improvement. He then did a fifteen-minute yoga session on YouTube and thought about how he'd tell Casey that he did yoga sometimes now. "We used to make fun of those people, but now? I see the benefits in my back," he muttered to himself now in preparation. He imagined that Casey would laugh with him and then say, "I've done a few YouTube videos myself... Getting older is something else, isn't it?"

What a privilege it was to watch someone you love get older.

Just past five-fifteen, Grant checked his phone again and reasoned that he still had many hours before dinnertime. Probably, he wouldn't give up hope till nine or ten, as he could envision Casey stewing in anger and fear in the Keating House, humming and hawing about what to do next. "Choose us. Choose love," he urged the window, as though it was a direct portal to Casey's room.

Just then, a knock rang out through Grant's hotel room. He jumped toward the door, suddenly fuzzy with expectation. But when he opened it, he found only the receptionist, who passed him a large manila envelope with a bored gesture.

"This was delivered here for you," she said, showing him her grey piece of gum between her teeth.

"Huh." Grant took the envelope and nodded firmly. "Who dropped it off?"

The receptionist shrugged. "Never seen her before." She then sauntered toward the staircase and left Grant alone in the doorway.

Grant stepped back into his hotel room as his heart thudded. He placed the manila envelope on the antique desk and tried to imagine what was inside. It suddenly felt like a ticking time bomb. Could he just toss it out the window and make it disappear? Could he leave the envelope untouched and take off for Hawaii, Geneva, or Melbourne?

With shaking hands, he opened it and slid out the very papers he'd dreaded.

He'd been served divorce papers.

How marvelous.

At that moment, his phone dinged with news from the local florist. The bouquet he'd selected for Casey was ready for pick-up. As he'd already paid, he decided not to answer it. The flowers would wilt on without either of them, as dead as their marriage.

"I'm going to take it," he'd told Casey about the job in sales. *"The kids don't need me anymore. You're about to take this big job in Sacramento. I need something to get me through the day."*

It had been only two years before Casey quit the architecture firm. Grant had planted himself firmly in the sales world throughout that time— and found himself admittedly, telling himself just how much he deserved his success. *"Marriage is about a partnership, and you've given your all. It's time for you to take something for yourself,"* he'd told himself. Was that selfish? He hadn't thought so at the time.

"I won't be gone that long," he'd told Casey over and over again. *"It's just so important to my career that I make this meeting. Nobody's ever needed my expertise in this way. I finally feel I've come into my own."*

He felt like a clown and a reckless fool.

Casey had never been gone for work as long Grant had been, not once in all her world-renowned architectural ventures. She'd always called home. She'd always texted goodnight. Grant hadn't. And why was that? He wracked his brain for some kind of answer, but came up dry.

A single purple sticky note was attached to the last page of the divorce papers. Casey's handwriting told him, "Get a lawyer, Grant. I'm serious."

Love you too, sweetheart.

Ten minutes later, Grant rapped his knuckles against the hotel bar. Frank raised his chin in greeting. His smile was the most genuine thing Grant had seen all day.

"Grant! Good to see you. The receptionist said that you're back with us for a week this time."

"We'll see about that." Grant's tone terrified him. "Can I get a whiskey? Double."

Frank whipped into action. Behind him, the television blared the sports station, which recounted the fascinating events of an NBA basketball game from the night before. Grant's eyes glazed over with the news. With his drink before him, he dipped his head back and sipped the first of what would be many sips. He was a soon-to-be-divorcée. He needed to wear the label. He needed to see how it fit.

"I'll have one with you if you don't mind," Frank said as he poured himself a glass.

"More the merrier," Grant replied.

Before long, Frank turned off the television and turned on the stereo. His favorite songs vibrated over Grant— taking him from T. Rex to Queen to Joy Division and beyond. Grant dropped his head back as a lull took over him. He imagined himself as a teenager, listening to these very tunes with Quintin, long before Quintin had become the once-iconic ranch owner, Quintin Griffin. When Quintin's fame had skyrocketed, Grant had done what any little brother might have done. He'd teased him about it. "Oh, look at the big famous rancher. Isn't he so big, rich, and strong?"

It wasn't so difficult to pinpoint when everything had shifted entirely in Quintin's life.

The day Quintin's daughter had fallen off the horse and died, the narrative had shifted.

What had been wild nights of partying and frenetic dancing and the pursuit of beauty and electricity and life had fallen away to nights of drunken weeping, overly reckless purchasing, and a loss of sanity.

Grant had watched it all with a mix of fear and sorrow. He'd always revered his older brother. He'd never envisioned such a downfall.

Around his fourth drink, Grant placed his left cheek on the cool wood of the bar and watched as the snow whirled outside. Frank said something about not usually allowing clients to drink as much as Grant did, but, "Heck. It's Christmas, isn't it? It can be the loneliest time of the year. And if there's anything I can guess about a guy like you staying around this little hotel as much as you have, it's that you're lonely."

Grant couldn't lift his head to answer. Frank clucked his tongue, as though he'd learned all he needed to know. Deep in his pocket, Grant's phone buzzed and buzzed, over and over again, until Grant finally forced himself upright and dragged it out of his pocket.

The name he read wasn't Casey's name.

It was Quintin's.

And for a long time, Grant wasn't sure he wanted to answer.

But when he did, he learned something that sobered him up almost instantly.

The voice on the other end was something to live for.

When he jumped up from the barstool, it collapsed behind

him with a horrible clank. He tossed a fifty on the countertop and thanked Frank for all he'd done.

"I thought you were sticking around another week?" Frank hollered as Grant raced toward the staircase.

Grant didn't have space in his mind to answer. He had to leave Bar Harbor. Maybe he'd never return.

Chapter Thirteen

Morning light streamed in through the enormous bay windows of the Keating Inn foyer. Casey swiped the dust cloth across the front counter, over the computer screen, and then, over the same spot again as her eyes glazed with the warmth of the December sun. It had been approximately fourteen hours since Rachel Marris had dropped the divorce papers at the front desk of Grant's hotel, and since that moment, Casey hadn't slept a wink. It was going to be over soon. As soon as Grant signed the papers, she would be free.

Nicole burst into the Keating Inn seconds later, dressed in her running gear and a pair of bright white tennis shoes. Her ponytail bobbed around behind her playfully. Only her face told a stoic tale.

"I just ran past the hotel," she said. "I asked the receptionist about him. She said he checked out late last night and took a taxi somewhere. His car's still out front, already peppered with two parking tickets. I'm not sure where he would have gone without his car? It's really strange."

Casey furrowed her brow. This really was weird. The real question here, though, was whether or not it was entirely her problem. As his soon-to-be ex-wife, she reckoned not.

"Don't you think that's strange?" Nicole rolled up the sleeves of her thick runner's coat and spread her legs out wide upon the thick foyer rug.

"Sure. I don't know." Casey was unable to meet Nicole's eyes. "I'm just glad he's finally hearing me. But it's funny, isn't it? Men only begin to take notice when you cut them out."

Nicole leaned forward so that the tips of her fingers ruffled against the tips of her toes. Casey's heart hammered in her chest, threatening to alert her true feelings to Nicole.

"You're much stronger than me," Nicole said to the floor. "I would be in a heap."

Casey excused herself to the back office, where she flattened her palms across Uncle Joe's old desk and inhaled as much oxygen into her lungs as she could. Her phone buzzed distractedly, and she yanked it out of her pocket fearfully. It wasn't him.

"Melody. Hi, honey." When she'd seen her daughter's name across the screen, she'd dialed the number on instinct. Melody was her lifeline.

"Hi! Did you see my message? The deal went through! I'm going to go to New York City in a few days and meet her. You must have seen that movie she did last year with Brad Pitt?"

Melody's voice zipped up and down, akin to a songbird's. Casey found herself taking up the necessary dialogue, words like, "That is fantastic, honey," and, "I always knew you would be great one day." However, after a strange, cavernous gap in the conversation, Melody seemed to get the hint.

"Mom. What's up with you? You sound like you're practically asleep or something."

Casey's throat tightened. Rachel Marris had recently suggested that one of the first ways of "handling the truth of divorce" was laying the cards out for the children. As Casey and Melody had always been relatively close, Casey had assumed finding the words to describe the horrible aching of her heart would be easier with her rather than with Donnie. She now recognized the immensity of that mistake.

"Mom? You're freaking me out."

Casey's tongue traced a line along the back of her teeth. "Your father and I have had some problems lately, honey. After some very deep consideration, we've decided to divorce."

The detail that she'd served him divorce papers at his hotel could be left out.

"What?" Melody's voice became a whimper. "You're... you're divorcing?"

Casey was reminded of a much younger Melody, who'd fallen from her four-wheel bicycle and slashed a long red scratch up her leg. The blood had oozed out and streaked down her little white tennis shoe. Melody had screamed, "Why!" like a Broadway star at the height of her middle-show sorrow. Casey and Grant had privately made fun of it for years, screaming, "Why!" at one another from every corner of the house. Melody had never caught on that she'd been the inspiration.

Casey tipped her weight onto Uncle Joe's desk. "These things happen, honey," she tried to tell her.

"They don't happen to you and Dad," Melody retorted.

"Honey... You're twenty-four years old. I thought you'd be a little more reasonable. This was a very hard decision to make, not something we took lightly. It's difficult for all of..."

How could Casey describe the idea that you could feel so, so close to a human while feeling as though you no longer knew them at all?

"I'm coming to Bar Harbor," Melody spouted then.

"What? Mel, no. You have work to do."

"Not for a few days. I'm packing my bag right now. I'll be there in three hours."

Casey grumbled inwardly as Nicole entered the office, bringing with her the faintest scent of sweat from her run. Casey yearned to protest again if only to keep herself in the cocoon of her decision a little longer. But Melody said she had to go so she could focus on the task at hand. Casey could practically see her flinging her face creams, razors, and specialty hair products into her little toiletries bag.

"Who was that?" Nicole asked as she sucked down water from her water bottle.

"Melody. I finally told her about the divorce."

"Ooph. How did that go?"

"Not well," Casey grumbled.

Nicole nodded firmly. Casey didn't have to remind Nicole that Nicole's divorce had sent a crater through her relationships with her daughter and son, which she'd only recently mended. Abby especially had blamed her for the divorce and stuck by her father's side until his inevitable abandonment after he'd begun to build a brand-new family.

"She's a smart girl. She must have seen how little the two of you spent together over the past few years," Nicole pointed out.

"Of course, but she's also our daughter. She saw what she wanted to see."

"That's always the story, isn't it?"

"She'll be here in a few hours, presumably to talk me out of it," Casey continued. "I can't wait to see what she comes up with."

Nicole's eyes widened. "She's quite persuasive. Remember when she sold candy bars in high school to raise money for the marching band?"

"Every single Portland resident gained weight that autumn," Casey confirmed with a funny smirk. "Candy bar wrappers replaced leaves on the ground."

Nicole laughed appreciatively. "I'm off to the house to take a shower and change before lunch. You okay at the front desk until Abby gets here?"

"Sure thing." Casey wanted to articulate just how little she knew what to do with herself in any context, including within her bedroom alone. At least at the front desk of the Keating Inn, she had to deal with other people's problems— lost room keys and dirty towels, rather than the creeping suspicion that she'd just destroyed her entire family.

Melody appeared at the top step of the Keating Inn and Acadia Eatery at two o'clock in the afternoon. She wore Gucci sunglasses and thick winter boots that traced all the way past her knees and a gorgeous bright red coat, one that contrasted the blisteringly white snow beautifully. She might have been a feature in a fashion magazine. Casey had never had such singular style.

But behind the sunglasses, Melody's face was hard as stone. Clearly, she'd spent the previous few hours stewing in fears and resentment. Abby greeted her warmly from the front desk, only for Melody to give her a curt nod in return.

Casey stepped out from behind the front desk to face her daughter. She felt like a gladiator entering the coliseum, gearing for battle.

Melody flapped a handout. "I don't want to talk about this here," she stated immediately.

Casey nodded. She brought her coat around her shoulders and beckoned for Melody to follow. Once outside, their boots crunched softly through the snow as they headed back to where Casey's car had been parked. The sunlight was impenetrable and unforgiving, and even a single glance at the snow left you blind for seconds at a time.

Casey pressed the UNLOCK button on her key fob and slid into the driver's side. Melody dropped down and buckled her seatbelt. For a long moment, even as they pulled back down the driveway, Casey had no idea where to take the two of them. It was something like fate that led them to a wine bar along the water, the one that often showed sports like ice skating and horseback riding and curling on the big television screens. This, in Casey's opinion, was a welcome relief from the big three: basketball, baseball, and football.

Melody sat across from Casey at the table and scanned the wine list. From Casey's numerous travels earlier in her career, Casey probably knew just as much about wine as Melody now did, perhaps even more. Still, she knew it was important to Melody to feel as though she knew more than her mother, what with her newly-found cosmopolitan life.

"I suggest we try this 2001 Cote de Rhone," Melody said breezily. "If you don't mind sharing a bottle."

"Not in the slightest," Casey told her.

Melody ordered the bottle along with two glasses of water.

When the server returned, he uncorked the bottle and poured Melody just a hint of wine to taste. Melody approved it with a little noise in the back of her throat. Casey could have laughed aloud. She felt as though she watched a different version of herself from twenty years before, at the pinnacle of her architectural career and unconvinced she would have anything but luck her whole life long.

"So." Melody clacked her nails over the table. "Will you please try to tell me as much as you can? You at least owe an explanation."

Casey stiffened. She then sipped her glass of wine, coating her tongue with the delightful depth of the wine's flavor.

"Your father and I have decided to take separate roads," Casey told her simply. "I want to focus on life here in Bar Harbor. I want to build a new Keating House next to the old one. I need a project, something to dig my fingers into and besides, you must have noticed how happy I've been here with my sisters and also how absent your father has been."

Melody seemed unconvinced. "I guess you seem a little bit happier than you were in Portland."

"I haven't been happy since my career ended abruptly," Casey told her, surprising herself with her honesty. "It was my passion. It was my life. Yes, I loved being a wife and a mother, but it wasn't what I always dreamed of, unlike others. Architecture always came first. And then one day, it slipped through my fingers."

Casey had never told Melody the real reason she'd quit the firm: that she'd followed her hot-headed temper directly out of the building and never looked back. This wasn't something she was proud of.

"But why is it now, either Dad or career? Why can't you have both?" Melody asked as her voice cracked for the first time.

Casey sniffed. How could she possibly explain to her daughter that she was borderline-convinced that Grant had lied to her for so many years? How could she tell her that Rachel Marris had suggested that he had hidden bank accounts and potentially another family somewhere? How could she describe the density of her broken heart?

"I have a very good lawyer," Casey said instead. "She's helping me through the intricacies of it all."

"And Dad? Does Dad have a lawyer?" Melody bristled. "I should have called him. Gosh, it looks like I'm taking sides now."

"You're just drinking a glass of wine with your mother. This isn't a war," Casey countered.

They fell silent. Melody took a longer sip of her wine and placed her elbows on the table like a teenager. Casey's instinct was to tell her to take them off, but she resisted.

"I just can't imagine you and Dad not being in love anymore," Melody breathed.

Casey's heart jumped into her throat. "I'll always love your father, in a way. But sometimes, I don't think love is enough. As terrible and as sad as that sounds."

Melody blew the air out of her lips. Casey recognized that this probably wasn't good fodder for her personal hopes that Melody would find a husband and raise a family of her own sometime in the future. That was another day's problem.

They got through their first glass of wine before Melody glanced up at the large-screen television in the corner. Melody's eyes widened to the size of saucers. She smacked her glass of wine back on the table as she gasped.

"Mom! Look!"

Casey yanked around to follow her daughter's gaze to the television. To the left of the screen, there was a very familiar face.

Quintin Griffin peered back at them. It was an older and less-healthy and sadder-looking version than the one who'd hand-selected Casey all those years ago to design his mansion and ranch, but it was Quintin Griffin, nonetheless.

Besides his face were the words: Rancher Quintin Griffin Attempts Suicide.

Casey leaped up to the bartender at the wrap-around bar. "Can you turn on the volume?" she blared as if her life depended on it.

The bartender did as he was asked. In a moment, Casey and Melody hugged the counter and leaned toward the television as the announcer described the events of the previous fourteen hours.

"Late last night at his Montana ranch, once-millionaire Quintin Griffin was found incapacitated after an attempt of suicide. He was rushed to a nearby hospital, where he was stabilized. As those in the horse racing and ranching communities know, Quintin Griffin was once a prominent and successful rancher and horse-racer, one who gambled and partied with the likes of other high-rollers and celebrities. Several years ago, his eldest daughter, Frankie, died in a freak horseback riding accident, which might have contributed to exacerbating Griffin's already-horrific gambling and alcohol addictions. It's been said that since then, Griffin has lost his enormous wealth."

Melody placed her hand over her mouth as a sob welled through her. The bartender glanced at them with confusion as the news station turned to commercials.

It suddenly clicked why Grant had had to leave Bar Harbor in such a rush.

He'd learned of his brother in Montana.

Hurriedly, Melody grabbed her phone and tried to call her father, while Casey stood with bated breath alongside her. Casey remembered all the months previously when she'd dialed Grant's number with lackluster hope. All she'd wanted was to hear his voice.

Now, Grant answered Melody on the second ring. Casey couldn't make out anything but the sound of his voice.

"Dad? I just heard about Uncle Quintin." Melody's voice broke with fear. "You're in Montana, right?" There was a pause as Grant filled her in on more details. "Okay. Okay. You know what? I'm coming there. I'll be on the next flight. I'll text you more details when I know. And Dad? I love you."

Chapter Fourteen

T he very hospital where Grant and Quintin Griffin had both entered the world was the same one the EMT workers had rushed Quintin to after his poor wife, Henrietta, found him in the bathroom after taking a deadly number of pills. Quintin now slept fitfully atop scratchy sheets in a single room, with a clear tube attached to the top of his hand. His lips remained blueish purple and sometimes, his eyes tossed back and forth behind his eyelids, as though the drugs had shot him into a strange dream state from which he would never wake.

The doctors had told Grant and Henrietta that he would awaken within the next day rather than linger on in this coma. "He was lucky," one doctor had said. "If you hadn't found him when you did, Mrs. Griffin, this would be a very different story."

Henrietta was nothing but skin and bones wrapped in a dark paisley dress. She dotted her nose with a handkerchief and stared intently at the wall. Grant had never been particularly close with his brother's wife yet had watched, helpless, as she'd generally closed up shop, mentally, after Frankie's death. Quintin himself had never been particularly kind to her, as he'd expected her to fulfill the old-fashioned category of "wife and mother." With their girls grown and one of them off the earth, Henrietta seemed like a tossed-out piece of furniture in serious disrepair.

"Melody will be here tonight," Grant told Henrietta as his heart lifted. "She's pretty dang worried about her stupid uncle."

The joke landed poorly. Henrietta dabbed her nose again and then rose to trace the path back to the bathroom. This left Grant in the silence of himself as his head continued to hammer with his hangover.

The call he'd received the previous evening while at the hotel in Bar Harbor had been from Quintin himself. He'd slurred his words and told Grant that he had *absolutely nothing to live for anymore. It would be better if I was just dead.*" Grant had recognized the seriousness of the situation and dashed out of the hotel as soon as possible, where he'd flailed a hand skyward and grabbed a taxi. The taxi's cost had been exorbitant, and the last-minute flight hadn't been anything to scoff at, either. Still, Grant had arrived in Montana around midnight, when he'd received the voice messages from Henrietta, saying that they'd taken Quintin up to the hospital. "It's really touch and go right now," she'd said through wails. "They don't know whether he'll live and they're not telling me much."

Around the time Melody's flight landed, Grant hovered outside the airport in a rental vehicle and rubbed his palms together to warm them. He texted Henrietta again to check-in, but she seemed unwilling to engage with him. He texted Izzy instead, who reported that there was still no sign he'd wake up that evening.

It was a strange thing to love someone who was so messed up. Grant had watched the entire lifespan of Quintin Griffin with a mix of awe and horror. This wasn't the conclusion of that, but it certainly felt like a monstrous climax.

Grant's beautiful daughter, Melody, stepped out of the double-wide doors with a pair of overly-expensive sunglasses atop her head and a cherry-red coat wrapped tightly around her little frame. She hovered on the sidewalk for a moment until Grant hopped out to greet her. Her smile went straight through him, warming him like the first rays of morning light.

He realized now that he hadn't seen her since July.

Suddenly youthful, Melody hurried toward him and wrapped her arms around him. He swung her around, as though she was that same little girl he'd helped raise in frigid New England. When he dropped her back on the sidewalk, her eyes glittered with tears.

"Hi, Daddy."

Did she know about the divorce papers? Had Casey told her anything?

Did she even know that her existence was the reason he and Casey had married in the first place? She was no idiot; probably, she'd done the math.

"How's he doing?" she asked finally as her voice cracked.

"He's still sleeping," he explained. "But the doctors say he'll wake up either tonight or tomorrow."

"Gosh." Melody closed her eyes timidly. "When I saw his face on the television screen, I thought I was living a nightmare."

Grant placed her backpack in the backseat of the truck and as Melody eased into the passenger side. Grant then jumped into the driver's side and cranked the heat as Melody rubbed her cheeks, shivering.

Back up at the hospital, Melody hugged her Aunt Henrietta and then headed into her Uncle Quintin's room to sit with him quietly. Grant sat beside her and tried his darnedest not to focus on Quintin's bloated, strange-looking face. When they re-entered the hallway, Melody spotted her cousin Izzy and greeted her warmly, saying, "Gosh, Izz. I'm so sorry." To this, Izzy just murmured, "It's so good of you to come."

Grant counted his lucky stars that his almost-famous, terribly sophisticated daughter found it within her heart to make time for her family. Somewhere in his past, he must have done something good to deserve this. He wasn't sure what.

Melody admitted that she hadn't eaten much of anything all day. They headed to the hospital cafeteria, where they ordered burgers, fries, and milkshakes and marveled that any hospital with any sort of commitment to health had such things on their menu. Armed with their sustenance, they sat across from one another as silence shrouded them. Grant placed his lips around the milkshake's straw and sucked up the chocolate goodness.

"When Quintin and I were kids, we always got milkshakes at this little place at the side of the road," he heard himself tell his daughter. "They were a quarter each."

Melody's smile was barely visible. "The other day in Brooklyn, I watched a girl spend nine dollars on a milkshake."

"Nine dollars? We could have bought a whole horse for that price back then." Grant tried a joke but felt it fall as flat as a pancake between them.

Melody bowed her head slightly. "I never really knew Uncle Quintin that well."

"It makes me sad to hear you say that. I always wanted my kids to know my brother and his children. I guess the distance got the best of us," Grant admitted.

"I always loved Izzy and Frankie." Melody pressed her lips together and contemplated the French fry between her fingers. "I think Frankie's death was the first time I really understood what death meant."

Grant shook his head. "The tragedy was overwhelming for your Uncle Quintin, I think. Everything changed after that. The partying got worse. The gambling got worse."

"The news today said that he's lost all his wealth," Melody said softly.

Grant dropped his eyes toward his still-untouched burger. How could he describe the once-brilliance of his brother to his daughter, now as they sat in the hospital awaiting his recovery from attempted suicide? It didn't stack up.

"I've always had an immense amount of respect for my brother," Grant offered then. "He was my hero when I was younger, always bigger, stronger, and more capable than me. He thought it was pathetic that your mother had this successful career while I played house with you kids."

Melody furrowed her brows. "That's ridiculous."

"It was a different time back then," Grant added.

"Not that different— and besides, wasn't Uncle Quintin the one who picked Mom's architectural design for the ranch? It was him who propelled her career forward?"

Grant nodded. It felt as though they spoke of a fictional story about characters he'd never really known.

Melody ate the edge of her French fry timidly. "When I saw the news' story about Uncle Quintin, I was with Mom in Bar Harbor."

Grant's heart felt squeezed. He nodded firmly. "I guess you know, then."

"I guess I do."

"I hope you know that I'm not happy about any of it," Grant breathed.

"Mom says it's for the best," Melody offered.

"I'm not convinced it is. But, you know your mother. She's..."

"Strong of will?" Melody suggested.

"That's a good way of putting it." Grant swallowed to try to loosen his throat. "And it's something I've always loved about her. I never imagined it would be our downfall." He hated admitting this last word but felt it was necessary, there in the white-washed walls of the hospital cafeteria, to verbalize the truth.

That night, Grant drove Melody back to the Griffin Mansion, where they collapsed in separate guest rooms in preparation for what was assuredly going to be a very tumultuous and emotional few days. When they awoke the next morning, Melody prepared them a large pot of coffee and rifled through the fridge and pantry to prepare omelets with cheddar cheese and red onion.

"I never knew you could cook," Grant stated as she slid a vibrant-looking omelet over his plate and dropped a dollop of sour cream over it.

"I had to learn how to cook on my own at some point," Melody teased. "I didn't always have my dad around in the morning to make me breakfast during college."

Grant laughed appreciatively. "I remember chasing you out the door when you were a teenager demanding that you eat something before school. You were so resistant!"

"None of the cool kids ate breakfast, Dad," Melody said playfully.

"That sounds reckless," Grant returned. "You know that breakfast is the most important meal of the day."

"You've said it about a million times, yep," Melody returned as she dug into her omelet. "I guess I've finally started to listen."

Around nine, the two of them drove back up to the hospital to find Henrietta, Izzy, and Izzy's child, Max, in the foyer, talking quietly. Grant greeted them warmly and received word that Quintin hadn't awoken yet. He then glanced toward Melody, who gaped down at her phone as she received a call.

MOM, it read.

"I guess she's probably worried," Melody said distractedly. "I'll just go tell her everything's okay and come back as soon as I can."

Grant nodded. "Take your time, honey."

Melody walked down the hallway for a few minutes while Grant shifted his weight and leaned against the hallway wall. Izzy passed her son a book and muttered that he should read at least two chapters before lunchtime. Henrietta tore at her fingernails distractedly and watched the clock. Grant had never been particularly illuminated with the love between Henrietta and Quintin. It seemed outside the bounds of reason that it was him and Casey divorcing rather than the two of them. But what did he know?

Maybe divorce was mostly inevitable unless you turned a blind eye to your unhappiness?

Was that possible?

He didn't want to believe it.

"How dare you?"

The whisper rang out from his right side, rasping and horrendous. He leaped up from the hallway wall to stare down at a stricken version of his daughter. All the color had drained from her cheeks, and her hands were drawn into fists on either side of her frame. She looked at him as though he was the devil incarnate.

"Honey? What are you talking about?"

Melody clucked her tongue. "I can't believe I trusted you. All these years..." She then turned on her heel and stomped down the hallway toward the double-wide doors, leaving Grant in a state of stunned shock.

By the time he got up the energy to follow her, he raced down the hall, only to watch her drop into the belly of a cab and speed out of sight.

Chapter Fifteen

Casey had just dropped a bomb. The phone call to Melody hadn't been her cleverest move, but in the wake of what she'd just learned, she had felt it a necessity. Melody had said she'd be on the first flight back to Maine, that now that she understood the truth, she would never darken a door in Montana again. "That weasel," Melody had called her father, a sentiment that echoed Casey's feelings about her own father, Adam. Generation after generation, men remained very disappointing.

Casey now stood on quivering legs in the foyer of Rachel Marris's law office as Nicole and Heather sat before her, their faces marred with heavy worry lines. A strange painting of a fishing boat hung on the foyer wall. In the distance of the painting, an enormous wave swept up from the horizon line, poised to crash through the boat and destroy it. It was a fitting image for a divorce lawyer's foyer. Casey's marriage now felt like the boat in the picture.

Only an hour before, Rachel Marris had called to say that her subpoena had pinpointed a secret bank account, which Grant Griffin had set up three years before. The account was linked to a woman named Alyssa Limperis, whose address was listed as just down the street from the house where Quintin and Grant had grown up.

It was difficult, just then, to gauge who this Alyssa Limperis might be. Perhaps she was a previous lover in Grant's life. Perhaps they'd rekindled things during one of Grant's frequent trips back. Perhaps they'd discovered that their love, once-lost, sizzled stronger than ever in their late forties. Casey's mind ran amok with every type of scenario possible. She had to shut off her thoughts and patiently wait, or she would go mad in the process.

Three years! Three years ago, he'd set up this secret bank account for this mysterious Montana woman! It seemed remarkable. Casey now counted out the various moments through their (admittedly little) time spent together.

Birthdays, Christmases, Fourth of Julys.

He had cuddled her close as she'd slept and brought her beautiful gifts from his trips and cooked up her favorite meals when he'd happened to be around. He had cracked jokes from his time on the road, showed off his new words in different languages (he'd recently taken on a good deal of Spanish), and teased her flirtatiously, in a way that had allowed her to believe that sometimes, they were still in love.

All the while, he'd had this other woman and this other bank account.

It was incredible.

Even still, Heather found the words now to say, "Maybe she's mistaken."

Casey scoffed. "I don't know about that. How could you be

mistaken about a hidden bank account? And it's too perfect. She's from his hometown, for crying out loud."

Nicole closed her eyes against the horror of it all. At that moment, Rachel Marris stepped out of her office and greeted them.

"I'm so sorry to bring you in here like this," she said. "I figured you'd want to know as soon as possible."

"Of course," Casey replied with a heavy sigh. "It's better to face the music straight on."

Nicole, Heather, and Casey sat across from Rachel Marris as Rachel Marris turned the large computer screen around to face them. This way, they could see the exact date that Grant had opened this secret bank account, linked that same account with Alyssa Limperis, and deposited a steady stream of funds into that same bank account, once per month, over the past three years like clockwork.

The funds equated to fifty thousand dollars per year or one hundred and fifty thousand dollars in total.

"I did some digging on Alyssa Limperis," Rachel Marris continued. "She's thirty-two, with..."

"Excuse me? Thirty-two?" Casey asked as laughter rippled through her. She could feel her skin start to crawl as the anger engulfed her.

"That's right," Rachel affirmed.

"At least she's not twenty-two," Casey tried to joke.

Heather grimaced.

"She has three young children, all under the age of five," Rachel Marris continued.

"What?" Casey cried, hardly recognizing her voice. "Three children?"

Rachel nodded as her eyes hardened. "I told you. I see things like this all the time. Worlds that men think they can create when their wives aren't looking. I'm terribly sorry, Casey. I really am."

Nicole wrapped a hand over Casey's and gripped it as hard as she could. Casey blinked down at the ground for what seemed like a small eternity.

All she could visualize, just then, was Grant with Donnie and Melody, twenty years before. He'd been the world's greatest father. He'd written down every menial event. He'd championed everything from vegetable-eating to tricycle-riding to picture-drawing.

Now, he assuredly did that with another woman, with another family.

"Three children," Casey repeated. "I just can't wrap my mind around it."

"You said he only spent about half the year with you at home in Portland?" Rachel asked for clarification.

"That's right. I guess I understand why, now. Three kids is a whole lot of work," Casey affirmed with a sniff. "At least now, he can head off and live his life with her publicly and not have to worry about it being a secret any longer."

"But why did he stay in Bar Harbor so long to try to win you back?" Heather demanded. "It doesn't make any sense if he has this whole other life."

Casey shrugged flippantly. "You know men. They never know what they want until they lose something."

Rachel's eyebrows rose. "It's a frequent story." She then cleared her throat as Nicole's grip tightened still more around Casey's hand, so much so that it threatened to shatter Casey's bones.

"I would suggest now that we go over the next steps of the

divorce proceedings," Rachel advised. "So that we're prepared for every angle."

A half-hour later, Casey stumbled back out into the swirling winter wonderland of downtown Bar Harbor. Nicole and Heather were hot on her heels, protesting how quickly she walked away from them. Five cars away sat the very one Grant had left behind. Just as Nicole had said, it was already lined with bright yellow parking tickets. Casey stood before it and blinked at the stupid air freshener she'd hung on the rearview mirror. If she remembered correctly, it smelled of "the ocean."

"I can't believe he's done this to our family. I hate him," she whispered, mostly to the car.

Heather and Nicole hustled up behind her and exchanged glances. Nobody knew what to say. Casey was empathetic to her sisters' situation. She wouldn't have known how to console her, either.

After a long pause, Casey lifted her chin toward the grey skies above. Damp dollops of snow landed on her cheek and her forehead and the tip of her nose. It seemed incredible that she could still feel something as tender and beautiful as a December snowfall. It seemed incredible that there was still something beautiful to know in this world, now that she'd learned the truth.

"It's so strange," she said finally as her eyes closed. "It's strange to think about marriage. About all the mistakes you both make and about all the ways you know one another, inside and out, for better or for worse. Strange that you can know their allergies and their fears and the movies they love the most— and still feel as though you know nothing at all."

Heather and Nicole collected themselves on either side of

Casey and burrowed themselves against her. Nicole's arms tightened around her stomach while Heather massaged her shoulder.

"The important thing now is that we have one another," Heather murmured.

"We never needed anyone else," Nicole agreed.

Chapter Sixteen

I t had now been twenty-four hours since Melody raced out of the Montana hospital and sped off in a taxi. Since then, Grant had called Melody's cell twenty-five times, Casey's twenty-seven, and Donnie's eighteen. Not a member of his nuclear family had answered. It was as though they'd collectively decided he'd died. It seemed fitting, here in the white-washed walls of the hospital, as he waited for his older brother's nurse to finish up the sponge bath and re-open the hospital room for visitors. The clock on the wall ticked forward. In the corner, Henrietta grumbled that she had to head home to check on the cat.

They were out of the woods, physically speaking. Henrietta seemed exhausted at the prospect of what came next. Her husband had very nearly succeeded in taking his own life. Would he attempt to do it again? Would he manage it the next time?

"I'll call you if there's anything you should know," Grant told Henrietta as she gathered her purse and made her way down the hallway. She seemed unable to bend at the knee these days and tip-toed toward the glass door.

Grant tried again to text his daughter.

GRANT: Hey, honey. It's Dad. I just can't understand what happened yesterday. It was so awesome to have you here with us. I hope you'll tell me what happened and give me a chance to explain.

Grant heaved a sigh and then composed another text. It felt like throwing darts and missing every time.

GRANT: Your uncle woke up yesterday afternoon. He was groggy for a few hours before he went back to sleep again. I should be able to talk to him more today. I hope I'll get a better read on his mental state.

GRANT: If there's one thing I truly believe in, it's that we have to help one another forward. We have to lift each other up.

GRANT: Love you, sweetie.

Quintin's nurse stepped out of the hospital room fifteen minutes later and reported that Quintin was "all set." Grant stood on shaky knees and headed in. Since yesterday, flowers and balloons and candy boxes had come pouring in from members of the community, and Henrietta had loaded them up on the side table. A red balloon was caught in the draft from the heater and banged against the wall gently but ever-presently. Grant longed to pop it.

"Hey, little brother." Quintin blinked his eyes open. His hospital bed leaned halfway back, and his chapped hands were positioned on his chest of his hospital gown. His purplish face had faded the slightest bit, as had his bloated cheeks. Even still, he was a shadow of Quintin Griffin's former self.

"Hey, big brother," Grant echoed. "How are you feeling?"

"How would you feel if you just had a male nurse give you a sponge bath?" Quintin tried to joke.

Grant lent him a half-laugh as he dropped into the chair nearest the bed. The brothers locked eyes for a moment as the air shifted between them.

"I know I'm the biggest screw-up on the planet, Grant," Quintin admitted finally, his voice cracking.

Grant's lips parted in surprise. He hadn't expected pure honesty this fast out of the gate. Tears rolled down Quintin's face and lined his lips.

"Tell me I wasn't always like this," Quintin murmured.

Grant furrowed his brow. The last thing he wanted to do was make Quintin feel worse. This was a fragile time and he had to think carefully of the words that would come next.

"You've always been an incredible human being, Quintin. I always looked up to you. You've just had a hell of a few years. Nobody could have seen that coming."

Quintin cleared his throat as his eyes grew blank. "It's true that things shifted when Frankie died. But dammit, I was on the way down before that, and you know it. Gambling right and left. Partying like my life depended on it. Henrietta threatened me with divorce more times than I could count. She doesn't have any idea of where she'd go, which is why she's stuck around this long. She took one wing of that big mansion while I took the other."

Mention of the house drew a direct line to Casey and the love Grant had lost. He shivered with sorrow.

"The truth is, Grant, I ruined my life, and I've been working hard to ruin yours, too," Quintin continued gruffly. "I've been nothing but a burden. I can see it in everything I do. And there's no reason for me to stick around and make everything worse."

Grant's heart seized. He reached for his brother's hand and held it gently. He probably hadn't touched his brother in years and maybe never this tenderly. He wondered why men weren't allowed such softness. Why did they always have to pretend to be so hard?

"When I gave you that black eye the night before Thanksgiving..." Quintin continued. "After you left, I just sat there in the silence of myself and got drunker and drunker. I think my grandson came in and found me and tried to play with me. I just turned him away. Is that the kind of man I am now? The kind that punches his brother in the eye and..." He trailed off. "I don't want to live like this anymore, Grant."

Against the wall, there was the same thump-thump of the red balloon. Everything seemed remarkably sad.

"You don't have to, Quintin," Grant told him. "You have to change your ways. There's no other way but forward. There will always be a brighter day, somewhere in the distance. We're all here for you and we love you."

He wasn't sure if he said the words to Quintin now or to himself. Regardless, he was pretty sure neither of them thought the words held any layer of truth.

Grant tried his darnedest to come up with something else to say, some other topic that would distract Quintin from the failure of his life and the failure of his death. Instead, after ten minutes, he said he'd run off to the cafeteria to grab them both glasses of soda. Quintin nodded and said, "I'd like that."

This was at least a start.

Grant stepped into the hallway and nearly ran headlong into

Alyssa Limperis, who carried a nine-month-old baby strapped across her chest while pushing a two-year-old and a four-year-old in a double stroller. Alyssa, who was thirty-two years old and had grown up just down the block from Grant and Quintin (a full fifteen years after Grant himself was born), had been something of a beauty queen around their Montana community, frequently participating in talent and beauty competitions and often winning them. Seven years ago, her long-time fiancé had died of cancer, and since then, her eyes had grown shadowed and far away.

"Grant! Hi." Her smile retained its electricity, its brightness, even as her lips quivered at the edges.

"Good morning, Alyssa." Grant gave her a soft side-hug and eyed the baby, whose closed eyelids were nearly translucent, blocking the beautiful blue eyes beneath.

"And how are you two doing this morning? You giving your momma a hard time?" Grant greeted the two-year-old, Greta, and the four-year-old, Dean, who gave him silly smiles in return.

"They've been very good to me today. Surprise, surprise," Alyssa replied simply. "Miracles do happen, I suppose."

Grant nodded sadly as they eyed one another. It was difficult to know what to say, especially as so many hospital staff members and visitors bobbed around them with inquisitive eyes.

"How's he doing?" Alyssa asked finally.

"He's okay," Grant returned. "I'm headed to grab him a drink. I'm sure he should only drink water from here on out, but—"

Alyssa shrugged. "Might as well give him what he wants right now." Her eyes dampened with tears that she didn't allow fall.

Grant's throat tightened. He glanced around as Alyssa's eyes widened. He wasn't entirely sure he was equipped to handle the intensity of this emotion.

"Henrietta went home to check on something," he said finally.

Alyssa nodded as her hand cupped the baby's head. She glanced toward Quintin's still-closed door as though she wasn't sure where to place her gaze.

"I hate saying this to you right now, Grant. I really do," she breathed.

Grant furrowed his brow. "What's on your mind?"

Alyssa's voice lowered to something less than a whisper. "I tried to get money this morning, but the ATM said the account was frozen. I went inside to ask the bank teller, and she said the same thing." Her eyes widened as fear permeated her face. "Don't tell me you're..."

Then, she trailed off as Grant's face contorted with sudden understanding. His lips parted in shock.

"You're out of money," Alyssa affirmed. "I should have known. I should have known rather than..."

"No, Alyssa. I'm not out of money," Grant returned in a cheeky tone. He reached into his back pocket and drew out his wallet, where he retrieved seventy-five dollars in cash and passed it over to her. "I'll get the account worked out. Don't you worry about that."

Alyssa furrowed her brow with confusion. "I don't understand."

"I have to run, Alyssa," Grant said firmly. "I'll be in contact." He then lurched down the hallway and sped toward the double-wide door, which kicked him out into the frigid air of a December day in Montana.

He almost vomited from the shock. How did everything end up this way? It was utter chaos!

How the hell had Casey learned about the account? Perhaps the lawyer she'd hired had done some digging? The world whizzed around him as his thoughts raced. He felt terribly dizzy. He stretched his hand out across the brick of the building where he'd entered the world, just a screaming baby with nothing to show for himself.

When Melody had come back into the hallway and said, *"How dare you?"*

It seemed obvious, now. She'd learned of the bank account. She'd learned of Alyssa and the kids.

God, he needed to get back to Maine as soon as possible. He reached for his phone and typed up a text message to Stacy, his secretary, with a request to book him a flight back to Portland. But just before he sent it off, he remembered that actually, he'd fired Stacy four months ago when she'd come on to him at a company party and he'd told her that that sort of behavior was inappropriate. *"I've wanted you for years, Grant. You must know that"* she'd sobbed as she'd packed up her things. This was a story Grant had shoved into the back alleys of his mind, as it made him feel guilty that he'd had to fire her. But he'd had no other choice.

Instead, he booked a flight for early tomorrow morning himself. With the ticket purchased, he dropped his head back and let out a wild, sharp scream. He'd never felt this far away from himself before. He'd never felt so painfully confused.

Chapter Seventeen

The morning of December 13th, Casey shook hands with Bar Harbor construction company coordinator Baxter Allen regarding her plans to break ground on the Keating property for what she now termed "The Keating House Part Two." Mr. Allen had called the blueprints for the new house "phenomenal" and asked where she normally operated as an architect. She informed him that she'd been out of the game for many years but "so hoped to get back into it soon." He responded that he had several interested clients who just needed "interesting architectural plans, mostly for summer homes surrounding Bar Harbor." Casey was intrigued and agreed to give Mr. Allen her business cards to pass along. Perhaps she hadn't lost her game, after all. Perhaps this was just a fresh chapter in the book of her life.

The previous few days had been a whirlwind, to say the least. Casey had learned that the supposed love of her life had another family that lived in Montana and he'd given them at least one hundred and fifty thousand dollars over the past three years. She'd also learned that the only way she could force herself through the darkness of this horrific time was to keep going. Thusly, she'd charged through twelve-hour days at the Keating Inn, occasionally offering her abilities in the Acadia Eater as either a waitress or some kind of line cook. Beyond that, she worked tirelessly on the blueprints, had arranged this very meeting with the construction company about the next steps, and had Christmas shopped until she'd nearly collapsed. When that wasn't enough, she'd gone on to bake five different types of Christmas cookies, attended a few spin classes, run through some aerobics, and stretched through hours of yoga at the nearest gym.

"You're a go-getter, Casey. You always have been. I'll give you that, girl," Nicole told her one evening, her face stricken. "Just don't push yourself so far that you break."

After the meeting with the construction company, Casey sped off to the gym for another spin class, where she sweated herself silly, fixated on the image of herself in the wall-sized mirror straight ahead. The spin class instructor hollered directions, demanding that they lift themselves from the seat and spin faster, stronger. Casey allowed herself to forget the inner aching of her soul. She allowed herself to breathe.

Casey washed herself clean, then headed off to meet Heather, Nicole, their cousin Brittany (Uncle Joe's daughter), Melody, and Abby. They all waited for her at the nearby wine bar, the same one where Melody and Casey had learned of Quintin Griffin's attempt at suicide. That had been either six days or a lifetime ago. Casey wasn't sure which.

Melody erupted from the table when she first spotted her

mother. She flung her arms around her, greeting her warmly as she said, "There you are! I was getting worried."

Casey's smile was overly bright; it felt plastic and false on her face. "How was your trip to the city?"

Melody had journeyed to New York over the previous weekend to meet with more potential clients, including the actress who'd just worked with Brad Pitt. Casey had been genuinely surprised that Melody had the strength for such a trip, especially after what they'd just learned about Grant. In Melody's words, however, they "had to keep going." Otherwise, it meant letting Grant win.

"We ordered the hot mulled wine," Heather said as she jumped up to hug Casey immediately afterward. "And I meant to say something last night, but that butt of yours... Those spin classes are really showing off. I might have to join you next time."

Casey blushed as she sat down. How could she translate that the spin classes gave her nothing but mental release? Maybe the elevated butt would help her somewhere down the line if she ever cared to date again. Just then, she was ready to denounce all men.

"I have some great news," Casey announced as she settled deeper into her chair. "The construction company approved the designs. They want to break ground on the property as soon as the ground thaws. We'll have a second Keating House mid-way through summer, I bet."

"That's incredible!" Heather cried.

"Now we just have to fight over who gets to live in the house you designed," Abby added with a vibrant smile.

"I want to stay in Uncle Joe's place," Nicole affirmed. "It's nostalgic for me now."

"That makes sense," Casey said thoughtfully, although she'd

never understood Nicole's affection for Uncle Joe. She'd tried to explain the friendship they'd cultivated, but Casey's heart remained semi-hardened to thoughts of Uncle Joe and Adam Keating.

"And then we can start the decorating process!" Heather continued excitedly. "Melody, I'm guessing you'd like to have a hand in that?"

Melody grinned wildly. "I have about a million ideas."

They drank through their first mulled wine and ordered seconds, along with two wooden boards covered with stinky soft and hard types of cheeses, plus plump purple grapes and sesame-covered crackers.

"This is perfect finger food," Casey stated with a laugh. "I can't believe I ever prepared any kind of meal for a man."

"They're always so hungry!" Nicole giggled. "Michael used to ask me what was for dinner every day around two in the afternoon. I was like, I don't know! I just had lunch!"

"My ex-boyfriend was the same," Abby, who'd recently gone through a hellish breakup of her own, affirmed. "I had to hide my favorite snacks to make sure he wouldn't eat them."

The conversation rolled forward as snow fluttered down outside. Although Casey felt vibrant and very much within the conversation, a small part of her surged with sorrow. Despite her never-ending workout regime and her constant striving to make the time pass as quickly as possible, a part of her knew she would never overcome her "love" for Grant. It was like a tumor she would have to carry around for the rest of time.

Nobody told you love was so debilitating. It was something you learned along the way, midway through your own personal destruction.

As Nicole sipped her second glass of mulled wine, her phone rang and she answered it with a splitting grin across her face. Heather and Casey locked eyes as Nicole said, "You did what?" to whoever had called. "You made a reservation? Are you kidding?"

Melody mouthed, "With that Snow guy?" as she reached for a grape and placed it delicately on her tongue.

"I can be ready by seven, sure," Nicole replied as her smile widened. "Just give me a hint. Is it fancy?"

"Yep. It's the Snow guy," Heather muttered toward Melody, who pressed her hand over her lips with excitement.

When Nicole got off the phone a moment later, the Harvey women at the table "oohed" and "aahed" to tease her. She blushed as she pressed her phone back into her pocket.

"I'm sorry to kill the mood," Nicole said as she whipped her locks down her shoulders, embarrassed.

"What are you going to wear for your big date?" Melody asked.

Nicole rolled her eyes as both Heather and Casey interrupted to say, in unison, "It's not a date!"

"Yes, that's right," Nicole exclaimed. "You took the words right out of my mouth."

Casey leaned back in her chair and crossed her ankles as Nicole spoke excitedly about her upcoming "non-date" with Evan Snow and what she might wear to such an occasion. There was electricity behind her eyes that suited her softness well. It reminded Casey of years before, when Nicole and her youngest, Nate, had lived in Casey's house for over a year. They'd called each other "roommates" and gotten into occasional fights about little things like leaving the laundry room light on or not sorting the trash correctly. Nicole had whittled away with each passing day, becoming smaller, passionless.

Now, that Nicole was a person of the past. These days, Nicole was a spitfire, apt to reach into the world and demand what she wanted from it.

Perhaps Casey could be that way again. Perhaps this divorce was a chance for a new start.

Chapter Eighteen

The downtown Bar Harbor Christmas market was in full swing upon Grant's return to the quaint little town. It had taken him a little while to return after his trek to Portland, where he'd stepped into the darkened hallways of the home he'd once shared with Casey and regrouped. Between long, scalding showers and nourishing meals (cooked in the same kitchen where he'd learned to cook for his children), he'd wired Alyssa more money from his personal finances, just enough to get her through the next few months, then called Quintin frequently to check-in, and also fielded Henrietta's text messages as she described to him, point-blank, that she would never see him again, as she wanted a divorce from Quintin. This was something Grant understood within the depths of his soul. Henrietta had taken Quintin's abuse for far too long. It was time for them to cut their losses at the age of forty-nine and head their separate ways.

On December 15th, Grant boarded a Concord Coach bus to journey back to Bar Harbor from Portland. The bus quaked to and fro as it snaked up 295, through Augusta and Bangor, before dropping back down to Mount Desert Island. True to its glorious word, Maine's December shimmered with light and snowfall, and the bus's radio sang out Christmas tunes between old eighties and nineties hits. A young girl in the bus seat just left of him read a chapter book for the first time, a fact she announced to him in a way that showed off that she'd lost both of her front teeth recently. This reminded Grant of Melody, who'd lost both of her teeth around the same time as well. She'd loved sticking her tongue in the gap. This was something fashionista Melody might never have believed.

The Bar Harbor Christmas market lined the downtown streets with food, wine and beer kiosks and little homemade craft tables. Vendors greeted Grant warmly, thinking he was a tourist, as they'd presumably never seen his face before. When he reached his vehicle, which was parked at the side of the road, he laughed aloud to find no fewer than eight parking tickets. "Thanks for the welcome back," he mumbled to himself as he collected the yellow envelopes.

Inside the little colonial hotel, the same receptionist with the clacking nails greeted him with a smile.

"I really never thought we'd see you again. But here you are! You have to be the most addicted guest to this hotel of anyone on earth."

"I just can't stay away," he confirmed as he rapped his knuckles across the counter. "Can I book a room for the next five days?"

"Sure thing," the receptionist replied. "Frank will be glad to have you back. Think he gets lonely back there."

"Well, it is Christmas," Grant returned firmly. "I guess it's the time of loneliness for many."

"Most others might say the opposite," the receptionist said as she passed over his large, antique key. "Here you go."

Grant decided to head into the hotel bar briefly to say hello to Frank. However, when he entered, he found that Frank wasn't alone at the bar. Rather, Heather's boyfriend, Luke, sat at the far edge, perched on a stool, nursing a mid-afternoon beer.

"Well! Look at who's back," Frank beamed.

But Luke looked as though he'd seen a ghost. He stood as Grant took a hesitant step forward, his eyes widening.

"Let me guess," Grant said calmly, with nothing to lose. "You think I'm a threat to the Harvey Sisters."

Luke's nostrils flared. "You knew who I was that first night of Thanksgiving, didn't you?"

"No, not exactly," Grant confirmed.

Luke and Grant eyed one another suspiciously. Frank placed three shot glasses on the counter between them and said, "There will be no fighting in my bar. I hardly get anyone in here to drink in the first place. We can't build up a reputation as that kind of place. Do you hear me? Now, get over here and take a shot. All together. Just like our friend Grant likes it."

Luke took his shot glass in hand, still eyeing Grant angrily. Grant lifted his shot toward both Frank and Luke, cheering them before knocking the shot back. It burned the top of his throat and forced his thoughts to slow. When he dropped his chin again, he said simply, "The first thing I want to say to you is this. There are many, many ways I made mistakes in my marriage to Casey."

"That seems pretty damn clear," Luke countered.

A strange stabbing feeling crept over Grant's chest. He swallowed to try to numb the sensation.

"Not one of those mistakes has anything to do with infidelity," Grant continued coldly.

Luke's lips parted in surprise. Frank crossed and uncrossed his arms as his eyes turned from Luke to Grant and back again.

"Come on, Grant. Sit with us," Frank said firmly as a way to break the silence. "Sounds like you've got a whole lot on your mind."

Slowly, Luke returned to his stool at the far end of the bar. Grant selected the stool that was five seats away from his. Frank leaned against the wall behind them and then adjusted the speaker so that an old Led Zeppelin song buzzed up over the airwaves.

Bit by bit, Grant described to Luke the story of his marriage to Casey. He detailed the moment they met at his brother's house in Montana, the rise and subsequent fall of her career, and his life as a "stay-at-home dad," which had made him feel a complicated array of emotions. "I started to travel more and more for work, as it made me feel great to be good at something. I felt like I'd waited my whole life to be good at something," he stuttered. "But I felt Casey and me drifting apart. Then, my idiot brother got himself into a number of horrible situations. My work travel necessarily lined up with trips to Montana, where I stayed with him and tried to get him back on his feet again. His daughter died; I felt awful about it. Guilty, really, that my life had turned out so well and his had taken such a nosedive. He even started an affair with a woman in our hometown that resulted in three little kids, none of whom he could care for. I've picked up the slack as much as I can for him. I mean, if I don't do it, then who will? But I know Casey. She's a volatile one. If I'd told her what was going on, she would have said..."

Grant trailed off as devastation took hold of him. He found it difficult to breathe.

"Casey's anger can be scary," Luke finally said softly, delivering his first words of comfort.

Grant nearly laughed at this show of empathy. "I love her, though. God, I love her. Now that she knows about this bank account and Alyssa, I just need her to know that I did it out of love for my brother. I know how difficult life can be. And I just feel so lucky that Casey and I still have our babies. They're safe. They're good..."

Luke heaved a sigh, then took a long sip of his beer. When he set it back on its coaster, he gazed at the golden liquid somberly.

"There's a chance this is all a lie, isn't there?" Luke stated with an ironic laugh.

"Of course. There's always a chance that a stranger at a bar will lie to you," Grant returned. "Frank? What do you think?"

Frank considered this as he grabbed them another round of beers. "I've bartended all across the state of Maine. I've seen my share of bar fights and bar proposals and bar divorces. I think I've seen it all, to be honest with you both."

"People live out their whole lives in front of you," Luke affirmed. "You must have so many stories you've never told me."

"How could I even scratch the surface?" Frank asked. He then bobbed his head from side to side as he considered Grant's situation. "I don't know why, Luke, but I have to believe the man. He's spent more time sitting sad and alone in this hotel bar than anyone else I've seen come in through those doors."

Luke groaned inwardly, then took a long sip of his beer. "I think I told you that first night that I'm an orphan."

Grant nodded, remembering.

"The thing about that is, it makes me a sap. I feel that everyone should always be connected. If you have love, I see no reason to give up on it, as a general rule."

Grant's heart lifted. Perhaps his luck hadn't run out, after all.

"All right. All right. I'm going to call her," Luke declared, almost grumbling it.

"Who? Casey?" Frank asked.

"Are you crazy? I don't want Casey to bite my head off," Luke countered. "Naw. I'm going straight to the emotional center of those sisters. If there's any one of them that might listen to you, it's..."

But Grant already knew. "Heather. Of course."

Luke snapped his fingers in affirmation. "The woman is mostly heart. If it doesn't get through to her, you're lost, my man. Lost."

Chapter Nineteen

The ingredient list for Nicole's upcoming Christmas feasts had grown receipt-long so that one-half of it fluttered off the edge of the table. Casey watched with her pencil poised above the blueprint for the Keating House Part Two as Nicole chewed at the edge of her own before ultimately falling forward and scratching out a whole series of what looked like herbs and spices. "Unnecessary," she muttered. "Nobody in Maine wants to eat anything Indian-inspired for Christmas." Casey could only envision a hazy ecosystem of various recipe ideas; Nicole was still hyper-focused on making a statement. Casey knew better than to interrupt her and instead turned her eyes to the blueprint, which needed just the slightest adjustments before its finalization. She was thrilled with it, thrilled that she would walk the halls of a Casey Harvey original within the year. Who needed the "Griffin" on the end of that name, anyhow?

Suddenly, Heather burst into the enclosed porch and plastered herself against the door as she gasped for air. Her eyes were unfocused, her cheeks violently pink. Both Casey and Nicole burst into giggles as they asked, "What's gotten into you?"

Heather wasn't keen on laughter, which was a rarity these days. She collapsed on the spare chair between them and removed her mittens. "I just did something I shouldn't have," she exclaimed.

Casey arched an eyebrow. There was no telling what this meant in Heather-terms. She kept her pencil in its appropriate spot and waited, sensing this wouldn't take so long.

But before she knew it, Heather burst into tears and turned toward Casey. Her ocean-blue eyes seemed deeper now than any body of water Casey had ever seen.

"I just saw Grant," Heather admitted finally. "He's in town." She then squeezed her eyes shut as her body shook with fear.

Casey dropped her pencil as her jaw dropped. "What do you mean? On the street?"

Heather shook her head. "He's been drinking with Luke at the hotel bar he's staying at. He's been there for a few hours. The two of them got to talking, and, well, he's explained to Luke that..."

"That what?" Casey demanded, suddenly stricken.

"That he never cheated on you. That it's a huge misunderstanding. That he loves you more than life itself. He never had an affair, Casey." Heather gasped for air as her forehead wrinkles grew deeper. "I don't know what else to say. I just know... that I have to believe Luke. He's no liar, honey."

Casey puffed out her cheeks as that same wave of anger and frustration washed over her. "He's no liar? But Heather, how long have you known him? Like five minutes?"

Heather bristled at this and straightened her spine. She turned her eyes toward Nicole, who kept hers down on her ingredient list. Obviously, she listened intently.

"It's just that you should have seen his face," Heather tried.

"Heather..." Casey's emotional insides whirled around like a tornado. Poor Heather. She'd married a remarkable man who'd left this earth forever. How could Heather possibly comprehend the weight of what Grant had done? Still, it didn't mean she had to trounce all over Casey's business like this. This was so typical; why had Casey expected anything better?

"What? Casey, what?" Heather demanded, irate.

"I'm just saying. You're so naive. So sympathetic to hogwash. All those children's books you write, no wonder you subscribe to emotion the way you do," Casey said then. "So, Grant told you a story that sounded true. What now? I'm supposed to just run back into his arms like everything is perfectly okay?"

Heather's jaw dropped. "Naive? Are you serious?" she demanded.

Now, Nicole lifted her chin and glared at Casey. "I don't think Heather would say anything to hurt you. That's unfair."

But already, Casey bucked up from her chair, prepared to hurl a million insults. How dare Heather barge into her world like this? How dare she speak to Grant when she couldn't comprehend the weight of loneliness Grant had created in Casey's world over the past few years? After her jump, her foot found the pencil on the ground and crackled it so that pencil lead scattered.

With the volatility of Casey's motions, Heather cried, "Don't worry. I'll leave before you can hurt me even more," then burst into tears and hustled off the porch. Casey moaned and splayed her hand across her stomach, her heart heavy.

"Just because you're unhappy doesn't mean you have to make

everyone else unhappy," Nicole pointed out, disgruntled as she gathered her ingredient list and followed after Heather.

This left Casey alone on the porch with a busted pencil and a busted heart. She collapsed back on the chair, no longer energetic enough to manage another notch on the blueprint.

After a long, heart-racing pause, Casey grabbed her computer from her nearby backpack. She wasn't a typical social media user; she'd never gotten accustomed to posting images of her children or snapshots that illustrated her accomplishments. Her profile picture remained the one of her and Grant from twelve years ago, which Melody had taken when they'd been out at Quintin's ranch. Casey had been thirty-four at the time. Her eyes flickered over the image as her heart surged with regret.

Then, she did something purely self-destructive: she searched for the name Alyssa Limperis. Within the Keating House, she heard her sisters' murmurs as they headed upstairs. Naturally, they spoke of Casey, words Casey was grateful not to hear.

Alyssa Limperis' profile picture featured herself and what seemed to be her newest baby, which she had wrapped over her chest. She leaned against a wooden fence as a Montana sunset beamed orange behind her. In every respect, in every way, she was beautiful and vibrant. Casey's heart sputtered with jealousy.

Alyssa didn't have any of her settings on private, which was quite rare these days. Casey clicked through her first few profile pictures to find her on a short journey through Alyssa's early years of motherhood. With three children under five, she'd packed a whole lot of emotion in just a short time. Probably, her living room was akin to a small village after a hurricane. Grant had always been the one to tend to the toddler messes while Casey had gallivanted off from one architectural site to the next. Grant was probably so grateful to have a partner in those menial tasks, now. It clicked.

Casey continued to go through the photos, her eyes scanning for some sign of Grant. He'd been gone every single month for an extended period of time for many years, and it wasn't like Alyssa was particularly careful about what she put online. (Often, what Alyssa listed was crass enough to make Casey question everything. Who was this woman her husband had fallen in love with?)

After approximately forty-five minutes of searching, Casey still hadn't discovered a single photo of Alyssa and Grant together — a curious thing for such a sloppy social media poster.

She had, however, spotted Quintin Griffin within several of the photographs.

This Quintin Griffin was a different Quintin Griffin than Casey had met all those years before. In the wake of Frankie's accident, he'd grown despondent and an alcoholic, which had resulted in weight gain and a bloated face. He'd retained some of his handsome features, probably only due to his arrogance, and in many respects, looked like a powerful and sturdy American man, the kind you'd want to latch on to if your world seemed hazy with fears and sorrow.

In three of the photos, Quintin even held onto one of Alyssa's babies with a look of pride and adoration. This was the cowboy Quintin Griffin— not the man in a loveless marriage who'd lost his eldest daughter in a freak accident. Maybe he'd reached out for whatever love he'd been able to find. Maybe this had been it for him.

And beneath two of those Quintin-and-baby photos, Alyssa Limperis had written, *"My whole heart."*

Casey's own heart surged with doubt at that moment.

It made no sense— the secret bank account, the endless weeks away from home, the lies. But then again, Grant had a pretty enormous weakness, and that weakness had and always would be his older brother, Quintin Griffin. He would do anything to protect him. Had she made a mistake?

Chapter Twenty

J ust outside the colonial house-turned-hotel where Grant had chosen to live out the devastating weeks after Casey's announcement of divorce, an enormous Christmas tree had fallen to the ground and cast its tinsel and bulbs across the sidewalk. Casey blinked down at it, reminded of long ago when she'd watched a hunter drag a deer through the woods. The tree looked defeated. Above, the downtown Bar Harbor speaker system spat and crackled with Bing Crosby Christmas tunes.

Casey ducked into the warmth of the hotel and smiled at the receptionist.

"Hi there," she greeted Casey with a smile. "Welcome to Bar Harbor."

"Hello." Casey's gloved hands gripped the edge of the desk. "I wonder if you could inform Grant Griffin that I'm here? I need to speak with him."

The receptionist's eyes widened. "That guy is the biggest drama we've had at this hotel since I started."

Casey cocked her head as the receptionist brought her piece of gum from one corner of her mouth to the other.

"But he just left a few minutes ago," the receptionist said.

Casey's heart sank. "Did he say where he was going?"

"He usually walks out by the docks at night," the receptionist told her. "Kind of freaky that he does that. It's so dark down there."

But before the receptionist could finish her sentence, Casey ran out the door and fled as quickly as she could, her boots tracing little lines through the recently-fallen snow. The run was no more than a quarter of a mile, but it might as well have been a marathon. When she reached the edge of the boardwalk, she collapsed forward and gripped her knees. It was a sure thing that her cheeks were fire engine red.

It was long past dark and eerily quiet on the boardwalk. The dock wood creaked against the rush of the waves, and only three or four boats lingered, latched with aging rope. It took Casey a moment to adjust to the black, but slowly she found the outline of the boardwalk out in the distance and its attached docks. And a moment later, the moon sprung out from beneath a fluff of clouds, illuminating everything.

Only fifty feet away, Grant stood— that sturdy Montana cowboy, misplaced here on the rocky coastline of Maine. He had shoved his hands deep into his pockets, and his lips were slightly parted as he took in the splendor of Frenchman Bay before him. He'd spoken so frequently of majestic mountains and glorious oceans and purple plains of majesty, the adoration of an American man who believed, above all, in his country. Casey's heart surged with love for him.

In a million little specific ways, she could still feel that same twenty-something cowboy in the man down the dock. The moment he'd marched into Quintin Griffin's old dining room, her soul had screamed a resounding YES, one she hadn't been able to ignore, despite her consistent fight for her career and her future. Perhaps that had been the universe, piping up to say, *"Wait a minute, Casey. Maybe there's more to this whole life thing than you thought."*

As though Grant could hear her anxious, swirling thoughts, he suddenly turned rightward to face her. His face erupted with shock. Casey shivered so immensely that she couldn't move her feet forward.

He intuitively sensed it. He would have to be the one to come forward.

She'd already run herself silly from the hotel to the docks. The exhaustion overwhelmed her. Could she possibly say everything she desperately needed to say? Could she take back all the horrific, sharp-edged words she'd already spewed? She'd served him divorce papers, for goodness sake.

Divorce papers. To Grant. The love of her life.

Grant rushed toward her so that the chilly wind from Frenchman Bay swept through his thick black hair. When he reached her, he stopped short as his cerulean eyes widened. After a long, pregnant pause, he finally breathed, "Casey? What are you doing here?"

Casey nodded as her stomach swelled with sorrow. "Hi, Grant. I think I've made a mistake, but I need you to clarify a few things first?"

"Oh," was all he said.

A single tear traced down Casey's cheek, which she immediately flicked off.

"I didn't have an affair," he told her firmly, as though he wanted to get it out of the way as quickly as possible.

Casey nodded again. "I know that, now."

Grant licked his lips, which Casey wanted to scold him for. It was far too cold; they would immediately chap.

"I hate what's happened to us, Casey," Grant lamented. "I hate that we've fallen apart like this. We have too much history for this to happen."

Casey's eyes continued to well with tears. Every muscle within her urged her forward to collapse into Grant's arms. Again, she reminded herself that she wasn't Heather Harvey; she wasn't prone to such emotions and didn't give them so much power. At least, that's what she wanted to believe about herself.

"Will you come have a drink with me at the hotel?" Grant asked finally.

Casey's throat tightened.

"I have so many things I want to say to you, but I don't want to do them here in the cold," Grant told her.

Casey squeezed her eyes shut as Grant traced an arm around her shoulder and guided her back toward his hotel. They walked in silence, for what on earth could they possibly say on the street as the Christmas crowds whirled around them? Grant nodded toward the fallen Christmas tree and said, "They really go all-out with Christmas here, don't they? About one hundred times more than Portland."

To this, Casey looked up at him and replied, "I hate to admit I've fallen in love with Christmas in Bar Harbor. It's truly a magical place, and I now understand why my father and uncle loved it here so much."

When they entered the bar within the hotel, there were five

hotel guests, many of whom traveled alone and nursed light beers as they texted on their phones. Grant rapped the bar counter with his knuckles and greeted the bartender warmly. "Looks like tonight picked up since I left," he said, referring to the surroundings.

"A big rush," the bartender joked. His eyes sparkled toward Casey. "What can I get you two?"

Casey ordered a glass of white wine while Grant stuck with beer. Grant then led her toward the back window, where they sat facing one another as a candle flickered between them. Grant splayed his hands across the table as he drummed up some idea of what to say.

"I don't know where to start in all of this."

"Maybe you could start with Alyssa Limperis," Casey suggested.

Grant bristled slightly, but his eyes didn't stray from hers. She supposed this was a good sign.

"Quintin was always such a pillar of that community," Grant began. "Helping people out when they needed it, lending money, which he had in spades, at least for a while. A few years before Frankie died, Alyssa's long-time fiancé died of cancer. As Quintin explained, he and Alyssa got to talking one night at the bar about their losses, about their grief, and they couldn't shut up. He said it was the real love he'd never managed to have with Henrietta."

Casey's eyes turned toward the table. She had witnessed the chilly dynamic between Henrietta and Quintin countless times; she'd always blamed Quintin for it, as she'd felt him to be sinisterly old-fashioned. Henrietta's place had, and always would be, in the kitchen.

"He never wanted to divorce Henrietta, especially not after

what their family went through," Grant carried on. "And the trauma of his bad marriage and the loss of Frankie led him to drink and gamble exponentially, it seemed like."

"This must have also been around the time that your work picked up," Casey pointed out, remembering.

"Yes. It was," Grant affirmed. "And I managed to stop by Montana quite a lot."

"I remember sometimes that it was a surprise to me when I learned you were there," Casey said softly. "And I ached with worry that you regretted ever moving with me to Maine."

Grant's face cracked open with sorrow. "No. I never regretted that. Not once." He brought his hands out on either side of him, gesturing to the bar, which seemed to represent the great world of Maine that they'd built together after all these years. It was laughably simplistic. "You, Melody, and Donnie were my world. I just always felt— felt so guilty about leaving Quintin behind. I missed him. I missed it all. And after all the things he'd done to protect me."

Casey nodded somberly. Silence fell between them as the weight of his words shifted between them.

"Now that Alyssa has these babies, what will Quintin do?" Casey asked.

Grant's eyes were far away. "I don't know. I've told both of them that I can't keep giving so much money. They understand, but I just don't know what's next."

"Three little kids brought into the world like that," Casey murmured.

"Oh, but they're just the greatest little kids, Casey," Grant countered.

Casey's heart lifted. She'd forgotten this about Grant: that he could often be the sunniest optimist. She coated her tongue with wine.

"I called your secretary when I couldn't reach you on the night before Thanksgiving," she said finally. "And she told me that you had a number of secrets. Lives I could never understand. It shook me to my core."

Grant's lips parted in surprise. "Gosh, Casey, I guess I didn't tell you. It was all so awkward when it happened... But Stacy tried to make a move on me a few months back. I told her no, of course. I'd never insinuated that we were anything more than employer and employee. We couldn't work together after that. I've kind of done my own secretarial work since then, as I haven't had the time to find anyone else to fill the role. I guess that was her way of settling the score with me."

Jealousy surged through Casey. *That beautiful, blonde, early-thirty-something had been after her husband.*

But this jealousy joined with gratefulness for what she had. Grant had stayed true to his promise to love Casey and only Casey, forever.

"I know the bank account was dishonest," Grant admitted now, his voice low and gruff. "It's just that, over the past five years of my career, I've tried and tried to prove to you that I'm good enough for you, that I'm good at my job. That I'm a prosperous life partner. Helping out my brother in that way seemed weak. I wasn't sure how to approach you about it. It should never have come to that, and I'm so sorry. So, so sorry." He then pointed to his eye with a heavy sigh. "I guess now you can guess where that black eye came from. Quintin was rowdy; he didn't want to leave the bar and go home. My mere suggestion that we call a cab made him flash his wicked right-hook my way."

"Oh my gosh," Casey breathed.

Grant splayed his hand over hers, now. This touch felt so genuine, so intimate. It was almost as though they were lying next to each other in bed, rather than in this foreign hotel.

"I have so much to think about," Casey said finally as her heart performed cartwheels across her diaphragm.

Grant removed his hand then. They continued to gaze at one another with wonder.

"I understand," he murmured.

"But stay in Bar Harbor. Please," Casey offered tentatively.

"There's nowhere else on earth I'd rather be," he told her.

Chapter Twenty-One

Later that night, Casey appeared outside Heather's bedroom door with a platter of freshly-baked chocolate chip cookies and two mugs of hot chocolate. Heather answered on the second knock. Her eyes scanned from the cookies to the steaming mugs to Casey's face. Her eyes were glossy and her cheeks rouge and gruff from tears.

"You didn't bake those yourself, did you?" she asked tentatively.

"I actually did," Casey told her. She didn't mention that it had been the only thing she could do to keep her mind off the chaos of her inner thoughts and all Grant had just told her. She glanced behind Heather to spot several white pages upon her desk, where Heather had scrawled out what looked to be a short story.

Heather noticed and blushed even more. "I got inspired tonight. I guess it's all that naive emotion."

Casey shifted her weight, still holding onto the cookies and milk platter. "Heather... what I said... was really out of line, and I should have never said those things. I am so sorry. Really, I have no idea what came over me. Being in touch with your emotions is a gift and I'll admit it. I've always been jealous of it."

Heather's long lashes draped over her cheeks. Casey was struck with the memory, for just a second, that Heather and Casey didn't share a drop of the same blood. Had the circumstances been different, they never would have met. That ignorant Adam Keating. Yet he was the reason this gorgeous creature remained in Casey's world, so in a way, she was grateful.

"Maybe you want a little snack to get you through?" Casey suggested finally.

Heather nodded and stepped back to allow Casey to enter her bedroom. Casey then sat stiffly at the edge of Heather's bed as Heather collapsed at the desk, crossing her legs beneath her. She took a cookie and lifted it to her lips expectantly.

"I went to see him." Casey ran a hand through her hair, then looked at Heather. "And you were right. He never cheated. It was a complete misunderstanding."

Heather dropped the cookie on the ground. It crumbled across the rug as Heather raced across the bedroom and tossed her arms around Casey, nearly spilling her hot chocolate.

"I knew it. I just knew it," Heather cried.

Casey longed to articulate just how "trusting" Heather was and that it wasn't always bound to be true. This wasn't the time for that. She was just as over the moon as Heather was.

Casey explained what Grant had told her thus far about Quintin, his drinking and gambling addictions, his sorrow over his daughter's death, and his subsequent love for Alyssa Limperis.

"His career has failed. He has next-to-nothing. And Grant felt that he had no choice but to chip in when he could," Casey explained.

"He should never have lied to you about that," Heather said as her eyes widened.

"But I kind of understand why he did," Casey breathed finally. "It's not like we had stellar communication. We drifted apart in a million different ways and my anger— well. I'm sure it terrified him."

Heather nodded. "It's like a storm."

"I considered that on the walk back here," Casey breathed. "I've always had this horrible volatility. Maybe it's finally time to speak to someone about it."

"Why not also look into couple's counseling?" Heather tried.

"You mean, attack every single problem head-on at once?" Casey asked, her voice lilting. "You mean, actually get emotionally and mentally strong to allow for a more beautiful future for both of us?"

"Something like that," Heather returned with a vibrant laugh. "Why not?"

"I guess it stands to reason that we're all learning and growing as we go," Casey said thoughtfully. "And that no matter how old you get, the journey's never really over."

Heather buzzed her lips. "Isn't that just the worst and the best thing? That life is this story we get to tell ourselves, and we're the ones who make up the plot points?"

Casey laughed outright. "There you go again with your emotional imagination."

"I'll never change," Heather told her.

"Please. Don't," Casey agreed firmly.

~

Midway through Casey's shift the following day, she sizzled with adrenaline and fear. A middle-aged woman with a gaudy engagement ring chewed her gum aggressively as she declared that her hotel room towels were "very rough," and Casey turned away from her, distracted, and lifted her phone.

"Excuse me? I'm talking to you!" the woman howled, something she would almost assuredly put on her online review, to the detriment of the Keating Inn.

But Casey just couldn't take it. Hospitality was a fool's game. It wasn't hers.

"Hi," Casey spoke into the receiver.

"Hi." Grant's voice was as deep, emotional, and far-reaching as the Montana sky.

"Do you have time this afternoon? I want to ride horses with you like we used to."

"Horses?" The woman at the front desk had never been ignored to this extent before. "What on earth are you talking about?"

"Uh oh. Did you piss someone off at the hotel?" Grant's deep laughter was endearing.

"I'll take care of it," Casey returned, joining his laughter. She then kept him on the phone as she turned back toward the woman and said, "I just had to call the towel manufacturer," she explained. "They're going to make a whole new line of towels, just for your bathing pleasure."

All the color drained from the woman's face as she tried to rustle up some kind of response. Suddenly, Abby appeared from the back office, seemingly understanding that Casey had reached the end of her rope.

"Excuse me, ma'am. I can help you right here."

"Did you hear what your colleague just said to me?" the woman blared.

"She's um. She's making a very important phone call. We've had quite a day here at the Keating Inn. I hope you'll understand." Abby turned her bright eyes toward Casey with a mixture of disbelief and humor.

As the woman at the desk continued to blare on about her towel situation, Abby mouthed to Casey: "Go before you make an even bigger mess."

Two hours later, Grant and Casey sat side-by-side on horseback as they gazed out across the frigid blue of the glorious Frenchman Bay and toward the peak of Cadillac Mountain. They'd wrapped themselves up in layers, which provided insulation from the wicked, whipping winds that surged in off the Atlantic. Years and years before, Grant had instructed a twenty-two-year-old Casey on how to ride. He admitted now that she hadn't forgotten a single thing.

They continued to ride, with Casey behind Grant as he clipped forward. He rode with the prowess of a man who'd been raised on horseback. She tried her darnedest to envision what their lives might have been like had they lived out in Montana the past few decades. Her mind drummed up an image of herself in a cowboy hat, which was borderline laughable. Grant was correct in one thing; they'd built a near-perfect life for Donnie, Melody, and the both of them.

Now, perhaps they'd have the chance to spend the rest of their lives finding balance. Perhaps they'd have the rest of their lives to truly know and love one another, without hesitation and without jealousy and without lies. Perhaps it was possible.

Anything was if you worked for it. Wasn't it? Casey had to believe that.

Casey's phone blared loudly in her pocket when they paused at a rocky edge. Grant's eyes turned toward her as she removed her gloves and grabbed her phone to silence it. The name on the phone gave her immediate pause.

RACHEL MARRIS - DIVORCE LAWYER

"Shoot," she breathed.

"What is it?" Grant asked.

She ignored the call and shoved it into her pocket again. When she closed her eyes, a small tear traced toward her chin.

"Hey. Casey. Hey." Grant sounded alarmed. "You can tell me anything. You know that, right?"

Casey pressed her lips together as her phone blared again. When she lifted it, she found that Rachel Marris tried again.

"It's my divorce lawyer," she said softly. Her horse clipped its hooves against the rocks beneath them.

Silence fell between them. In the distance, a bird, leftover after countless migrations, cawed out across the sky.

"I would understand if you still wanted to go through with it," he told her softly. "There's been so much deceit and emptiness between us. If you want this fresh start in Bar Harbor— I mean, I had so much time, to be honest with you. I had so many opportunities to be home more. I..." He shook his head tentatively, unable to finish his sentence.

Casey's tongue tasted sour. She again shoved her phone back into her pocket, then directed her reins leftward to take them deeper along the mountain trail. Just before she yanked away, she said, "Maybe we could get dinner tomorrow night and talk about it more. But right now, I just want to live in the beauty of the Acadia Mountains. And I don't want to do it with anyone else but you."

Chapter Twenty-Two

M elody and Donnie arrived back to Bar Harbor the
following afternoon at two, an event that found Casey
hard at work in the kitchen of the Keating House, baking crois-
sants and Christmas cookies and brewing up hot mulled wine. She
wasn't needed at the Keating Inn, not today, nor any other day in
the near future (thankfully). After Casey's incident with the ritzy
towel woman, Nicole had requested that she "keep a wide berth"
of the Keating Inn, at least until after her "situation" was under
control. Nicole, Heather, and Abby hired a spontaneous stand-in
front-desk employee to take over Casey's shifts, and Casey had
burrowed herself into her sizzling emotions and enough cookie
dough to feed a small village. By the time her children arrived at
the Keating House, she was half-drunk and over-sugared. She
flung her arms around them as she shrieked with more joy than
she'd experienced in years.

Her entire family was in Bar Harbor. Every person she'd ever
really loved could be found within the city limits. Beyond that, she

was on the verge of breaking ground on the first building she'd designed in many years. After everything that had just happened, this was some kind of Christmas miracle.

"Mom..." Donnie hugged his mother extra long before she pulled back. His eyes were wounded.

"I just told Donnie everything in the car ride on the way here..." Melody offered finally. "I figured it was easier to just get it out of the way. I hope that's okay."

Donnie grabbed three Christmas cookies and collapsed at the kitchen table. Little shadows appeared beneath his eyes as he contemplated his father's affair and his parent's divorce. Casey sucked another sip of mulled wine down her throat as she considered how to tell them the newest plot points in what seemed to be this winter's wildest story.

"I just can't believe he was out in Montana with this whole other family," Donnie muttered in disbelief between big bites of his cookie.

"Obviously, neither of us have been in contact with him," Melody blared now as she flipped her hair. "He's probably been up in Montana just living out his days with his newfound family." Her voice was taut with anger.

Casey recognized her temper within Melody's. How she prayed that her children wouldn't have to live with the sort of anger that brewed within Casey. It was a curse.

"Kids... I have something to tell you," Casey announced suddenly, surprising herself with the gentleness of her tone.

Melody arched an eyebrow in surprise. She took the chair beside Donnie, wordless, as Casey wrapped her hands around her warm mug of hot mulled wine and tilted her head.

"Your father isn't in Montana. He's right here in Bar Harbor," she said.

Melody's jaw dropped open. Donnie chewed contemplatively on his Christmas cookie.

"What are you talking about? Does he really think he can just stomp back into your life after all he did?" Melody demanded.

"It's a bit more complicated than that," Casey tried.

"How, exactly?" Melody asked. She crossed and uncrossed her arms and blinked at her mother in disbelief.

"Well…" Casey blinked wildly as tears formed in her eyes. Donnie stood back up on instinct, as though he could protect his mother from her own emotions. It was no use. The tears came, hot and fast and in perfect succession. "It turns out your father never had an affair."

"But the bank account? The secretary?" Melody demanded.

Casey shook her head ever-so-slightly. "Your father worked tirelessly to cover up for his brother's mistakes."

"Uncle Quintin?" Donnie demanded, shock washing over his face.

"He lost everything since Frankie died," Casey explained. "Your father couldn't bear to see him collapse like that. He gave all he could. And in the process, he lost the world he loved the most. Ours."

Melody leaped up to join her brother and mother as her own eyes filled with tears. She fell against her mother and erupted with sobs of her own. Her anger had only been a facade, protection from her deep-rooted, swirling sorrows.

"I just didn't want to believe it," Melody whispered into her mother's shoulder. "I never wanted to think my dad was a bad guy."

Casey rubbed her daughter's shoulder as Donnie rubbed his

eyes till they turned bright pink at the edges.

"Your dad gave his all to be your dad," she whispered now. "While I ran all over, building my career, your dad was there for every moment of your early days, no matter how small or how big. He's always been an amazing man, an amazing father and I should have never doubted him. He loves you both more than life itself and although sometimes I feel I don't deserve his love, he still gives it to me— all these years later."

There was a great deal more to explain. Casey herself wasn't entirely sure where to start. Throughout the rest of the afternoon, she and her children sat in earnest at the kitchen table as she walked them through what she now understood about their Uncle Quintin and his new family with Alyssa Limperis and their three children, Melody and Donnie's adorable cousins. She also talked in greater detail about her and Grant's lack of communication over the years, along with Grant's desire to make something of himself after all his years as a "stay-at-home" dad. It was a complicated story with many moving parts. The best of it was, the story wasn't over yet.

Grant agreed to meet Casey at the Italian restaurant, "Calvino's," that evening at seven-thirty. Casey, Melody, and Donnie arrived fifteen minutes later to ensure the surprise. When Grant walked in with a bouquet of red roses, his smile broke open at the sight of his children. Melody rushed toward him and flung her arms around him as she cried, "Daddy!" Donnie fell into a big, burly hug immediately afterward. By the time Grant reached Casey, his one and only love, his eyes were heavy with tears.

"You brought my kids back to me," he whispered.

"They didn't want to be anywhere else but right here," she told him.

They kissed so deeply that Casey's knees almost gave out beneath her. When her eyes closed, she felt she'd dropped back in time to those early days when they were so deep in love, only to lurch back to 2021 when her eyes flipped back open.

The following hours were mesmerizing in their warmth. Grant, Casey, Melody, and Donnie hadn't sat together at a table as a family in more than a year. This newfound belief in their nuclear family resulted in non-stop conversation, wild banter and laughs from all corners— all with Casey and Grant holding hands across the table. At various times, Donnie and Melody gave one another knowing looks. It seemed they were convinced of their parents' newfound love.

Back outside the Italian restaurant, the snow swirled around them with expectant Christmas magic. Donnie told Grant excitedly about Thanksgiving and the multiple rounds of karaoke and charades Grant had to look forward to. Grant guffawed and then promised to sing ABBA's "Super Trooper." Donnie said he'd sing back-ups.

After a strange, hesitant pause, Casey shifted her head back toward the Keating Property. "Why don't you come up to the house for the night? We've got more Christmas cookies than we know what to do with."

Grant's face cracked into a huge smile. She could see a look of happiness wash over him at that moment and it warmed her heart.

"Let me just grab some stuff at the hotel," he replied, his eyes glittering as though this was all too good to be true. "There's nowhere else I'd rather be."

Chapter Twenty-Three

G rant awoke as the soft light of Christmas morning swept over his and Casey's antique bed in the corner bedroom of the Keating House. Casey stirred gently beside him as he curled around her petite frame and placed his hand across her stomach. He inhaled the lavender scent of her lotion and allowed himself to ease deeper into the mattress. It was only seven o'clock; there was still time to cherish the beauty of this moment. There was still time to breathe in the sincere pleasure of all he'd been given.

Since Grant's arrival back into the arms of his greatest love, he'd felt free from previous anxieties. His troubles with sleep had fallen away. His self-hatred had diminished. And his love for Bar Harbor and the other Harvey Sisters had only blossomed.

When Casey awoke a few minutes later, she turned into him so that her nose dipped against the tip of his.

"Good morning," she breathed.

"Merry Christmas." He wrapped both hands along the base of her back and held her close against him.

"Do you think Santa came?" she asked, then erupted with a yawn.

Grant laughed brightly. "I don't know about that. But I think I smell Nicole already baking up some cinnamon rolls, which in my world is much better than Santa Claus."

"What world do you come from exactly, Cowboy?" Casey teased.

"I've come from the Wild, Wild West," he replied in a deep baritone voice. "You know that."

"And what are you doing in the civilized state of Maine, Cowboy?"

Grant laughed so that the bed shook beneath them. "I met a beautiful girl. She cleaned me up and moved me out east, and I've hardly darkened the door of a saloon since."

Casey kissed him with her eyes closed, something he watched her do before he, too, closed his eyes and indulged in the beautiful texture of having loved the same person for nearly twenty-five years. It was a miraculous thing.

Casey and Grant donned their cozy robes, which they'd stolen from the Keating Inn, and headed downstairs to the sun-drenched kitchen to find Nicole, Heather, Bella, and Abby. Nicole was, in fact, hard at work on cinnamon rolls, while Bella, Abby, and Heather were hard at work on mimosas and plenty of gossip.

Grant's beautiful daughter breezed in a moment later and kissed her father on the cheek. "Merry Christmas, Daddy!" she called out. Her words pulled Grant all the way back to twenty years before. Time wasn't so gentle with any of us, he thought now. Melody poured the three of them new mimosas and greeted her mother with a hug.

"I like your robes!" Melody cried.

Nicole sniffed. "I have a hunch where you nabbed those from."

"I've been told not to stand at the front desk of the Keating Inn until I can put my hospitality hat back on," Casey said with a mischievous laugh. "What Nicole doesn't know is that I lost my hospitality hat."

Nicole grumbled playfully as she splayed several cinnamon rolls with thick frosting on a large platter. "I guess you've got your own stuff to focus on these days, anyway."

"That's right!" Grant said enthusiastically. "Casey, have you told your sisters the news?"

"Oh my god. You're pregnant," Heather said, her eyes bulging.

"Omg, girl," Casey returned. "No. It's just..." She paused, both for dramatic effect and to drive her sisters crazy. Grant knew her ways all too well. "I just received word from this business-woman in Spain. She's seen several of the buildings I designed around the world and has absolutely no idea why I haven't designed anything in the past few years. She put up a wealthy sum for me to design a series of hotels just outside of Barcelona. It's kind of a dream come true, as Barcelona has a pretty sincere commitment to architecture."

"Mom! Are you flipping kidding me?" Melody danced with excitement for her mother.

The kitchen erupted with joy. Nicole rushed forward to give Casey a cinnamon-sugar-and-frosting-coated hug. Heather burst into tears as she kissed Casey on the cheek.

"You're such a sincere talent, Aunt Casey," Abby compli-mented as she clasped her fingers together. "I've always been in awe of you."

Suddenly, Grant lifted his mimosa glass skyward and said, "I think it's time for a toast to all the Harvey Sisters— to the very best chef, the best writer, and the best architect, all wrapped up in one close-knit family."

"Well, kind of..." Heather interjected with a funny wink.

"There's no getting out of this family, Heather," Casey told her boldly. "We've told you that time and time again."

"No matter how much you might want to disown us sometimes," Nicole affirmed.

"To the Harvey Sisters!" Another voice chimed in from the foyer, just before the door clipped closed behind. Luke stepped through as he unraveled his scarf. "If you grab me a mimosa, I'd love to join this toast."

His surprise sent Heather into a state of chaos. While Melody poured him a glass, Heather flung her arms around his neck and kissed him directly on the mouth. When she tipped her head back, her ocean-blue eyes pooled with light.

"I'm not sure how any of us got this lucky," Casey whispered into Grant's ear, just softly enough so as not to be heard by any of the others. "I suppose it's some kind of Christmas miracle."

Grant shook his head delicately so that the tip of his nose nudged hers yet again. He was suddenly reminded of those hundreds and hundreds of nights he'd spent, latched away in nameless hotel rooms, watching news channels in cities he'd now long-forgotten the names of. He was no longer a man on the hunt for some kind of success he couldn't fully name.

This was his home— here with the eldest Harvey Sister and the great love of his life, on the rocky coastline of Maine. Nothing else in the world had ever truly mattered. He knew now to hold his love close, to cling to it for dear life. Time always tried its hardest to play tricks on you, but that was something you just couldn't let happen.

"Merry Christmas, Casey Harvey Griffin," he whispered now. "I've always loved you and can't wait to spend another twenty-five years with you. You're the greatest gift I've ever known."

Coming Next in the Bar Harbor

New Horizon in Bar Harbor

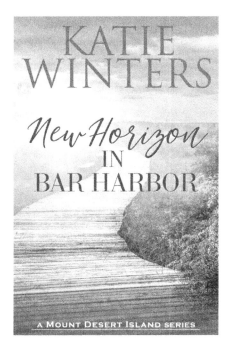

Other Books by Katie

The Vineyard Sunset Series

Secrets of Mackinac Island Series

Sisters of Edgartown Series

A Katama Bay Series

A Mount Desert Island Series

Connect with Katie Winters

BookBub: www.bookbub.com/authors/katie-winters
Amazon: www.amazon.com/Katie-Winters/e/B08B1S7BBN
Facebook: www.facebook.com/authorkatiewinters/
Newsletter: www.subscribepage.com/kwsiguppage

To receive exclusive updates from Katie Winters please sign up to be on her Newsletter!

www.subscribepage.com/kwsiguppage

27202214R00115